D1076717

0045300305

SPECIAL MESSAGE TO READERS

This book is published under the auspices of

THE ULVERSCROFT FOUNDATION

(registered charity No. 264873 UK)

Established in 1972 to provide funds for research, diagnosis and treatment of eye diseases. Examples of contributions made are: —

A Children's Assessment Unit at Moorfield's Hospital, London.

•

Twin operating theatres at the Western Ophthalmic Hospital, London.

•

A Chair of Ophthalmology at the Royal Australian College of Ophthalmologists.

•

The Ulverscroft Children's Eye Unit at the Great Ormond Street Hospital For Sick Children, London.

You can help further the work of the Foundation by making a donation or leaving a legacy. Every contribution, no matter how small, is received with gratitude. Please write for details to:

THE ULVERSCROFT FOUNDATION,
The Green, Bradgate Road, Anstey,
Leicester LE7 7FU, England.
Telephone: (0116) 236 4325

In Australia write to:
THE ULVERSCROFT FOUNDATION,
c/o The Royal Australian and New Zealand
College of Ophthalmologists,
94-98 Chalmers Street, Surry Hills,
N.S.W. 2010, Australia

DEVIL'S PEAK

Stranded in a High Peak transport café during a freak snowstorm, Jerry Howard finds himself in a vortex of Satanism. Brenda was a motorway girl with a strange scar on her back. The Mark of the Beast. She knew the history of the Brindley legend. And she alone knew the rites. She had been on Devil's Peak before. Now it was Walpurgisnacht and the horned goat was expected. Events moved to a horrendous climax . . .

Books by Brian Ball
in the Linford Mystery Library:

DEATH OF A LOW HANDICAP MAN
MONTENEGRIN GOLD
THE VENOMOUS SERPENT
MALICE OF THE SOUL
DEATH ON THE DRIVING RANGE

BRIAN BALL

◆

DEVIL'S PEAK

45 5/09 Property of Stockton Borough Libraries

0045300305

Complete and Unabridged

LINFORD
Leicester

First published in Great Britain

First Linford Edition
published 2009

Copyright © 1972 by Brian Ball
All rights reserved

British Library CIP Data

Ball, Brian, *1932* –
   Devil's Peak.—Large print ed.—
Linford mystery library
1. Murder—Investigation—Fiction
2. Suspense fiction 3. Large type books
I. Title
823.9'12 [F]

ISBN 978–1–84782–566–7

Published by
F. A. Thorpe (Publishing)
Anstey, Leicestershire

Set by Words & Graphics Ltd.
Anstey, Leicestershire
Printed and bound in Great Britain by
T. J. International Ltd., Padstow, Cornwall

This book is printed on acid-free paper

1

Jerry Howard knew he'd been the worst kind of fool when he saw the first black clouds screaming in from the northwest to blot out the High Peak.

In what was left of the pale spring sunlight, he could see the sheep alongside the Hagthorpe village road calling to their zany lambs as they made for cover.

'Oh, Christ,' he said, looking up. He was in deep trouble. There was the face of Devil's Peak leering at him, as if it knew that he was stuck, with the top of Toller Edge above seven or eight handholds away. It might as well have been in Outer Mongolia or Bangkok or in the Snug at the *Furnaceman's Arms,* which was where he wished himself now, instead of waiting with freezing hands for the courage to move up the vertical corner in the rock face.

M. Severe, the handbook had called the climb, which was named after

1

someone called Scragg — Scragg's Corner. Half an hour before Jerry had grinned to himself, made sure that his small rucksack was firmly in place on his back, and begun the ninety-foot ascent. Only fools climbed alone, of course, but this wasn't a real test of skill.

Anyway, who else could find time on a Friday at the end of the Easter vacation to go with him? Only Debbie, and she'd gone in a rage the week before, back to South Shields and the trawler captain who'd been waiting three months for her to get over what he called the Bearded Wonder. So Jerry had come out on his own. Well, so he'd done a small climb. Why not? You had to balance the thrill of doing the corner crack alone against the dangers — and he had done this particular climb three or four times before, so where was the danger? It wasn't until he was within twenty feet of the top that he'd found his fingers slipping on the gritstone and realised that there had been a sudden drop in the temperature.

It was seeing newly broken gritstone where there should have been a jug of rock that frightened him into looking round. Someone had done the unthinkable. Some vandal had come up Scragg's Corner and taken a hammer to the one handhold vital to the climb.

'Mad bastard!' Jerry exclaimed, aghast when he looked up to see why his icy fingers hadn't found the four-inch projection.

Who could have done it!

Some maniacal yob out with his mates after shooting up the daft sheep? A climber? But climbers wouldn't! It was totally unthinkable!

Jerry tried again and his fingers slid over wet, cold, smooth rock. And then he looked all about him with a sickening sense of danger. He had no top rope. No rope at all, in fact. He couldn't be hauled ignominiously to the top of Toller's Edge to be laughed at by his fellow-climbers. There weren't any. Nor could he go down a rope which he might have fixed to the rock himself. He'd been a fool. And it was getting so cold that his face stung abominably and his right hand jumped with frozen fatigue. He looked down, careful to keep both feet evenly balanced, left on a solid ledge, the other on a bit of rock that was no more than a slippery protuberance about the size and shape of a slice of orange. Below, the sunlight was dying. Last year's bracken had been trampled by the sheep in places, though it still lay thickly in a brown carpet. A tanker's air-brakes squealed on the narrow road at the turn for Hagthorpe.

Then Jerry sensed rather than saw the blackness that was looming over the High Peak. He did look then. Snow-clouds were roaring like banshees over the roof of England.

Snow!

The wind got up, adding an urgency to the sheep's calls. Jerry looked all about the Edge in case someone should have come out for a walk, or some party of climbers he hadn't noticed before were about. No one. Even the youngest of the kids who lived just below the broad bald masses of the Peak knew what the black clouds meant and would have turned for home double quick. A car ground its way along the Hagthorpe road, its driver

4

intent on getting to his destination.

The first snowflake drifted to settle in Jerry's dark beard as the sunlight was extinguished. He looked over his left shoulder towards Sheffield, where at the edge of the cloud belt there was still dazzling sunshine.

He shuddered as another snowflake landed on his nose and gently dissolved. He knew he could not stay still for much longer. *Go down?* He'd never make it. He was committed now. Below was a jumbled mass of rock eroded from the cliff-face. Not much more than sixty feet. Say seventy. Enough to break every bone in his body on the jagged edge of the harsh boulders. He called out above the wind:

'Help! On the Edge! Can't move!'

The wind filled his mouth as he roared, and the chill of it bit into a top filling of white metal. He shut his mouth quickly and thought of the unfairness of it all.

It was lonely in the bedsitter without Debbie's sing-song tones, so he had packed a pound of cheese and a small Hovis, stolen a couple of cans of beer from Andy and Anne's flat — knowing that they would have helped themselves just as freely from his — and set off to think out how he was to cajole another year's grant from his local education authority. That, and to do a spot of scrambling. Not *climbing,* he had told himself. Only fools climbed alone. And they didn't do it for long. Hagthorpe Cemetery held a couple at least.

Again the wind licked at his white metal filling. Snowflakes danced towards him, thrown there by some freak of wind from the High Peak. Above, the clouds were now solidly black.

The rock was getting more and more slippery as the snow began to settle in cracks and fissures, on tiny ledges and even on the vertical face itself until it was blown away over the top of Toller Edge twenty feet above. *Twenty feet!*

He reached out his right hand again and felt the raw new stone. A black rage filled him. Who could have been so cold-bloodedly murderous as to destroy the route up the corner? Jerry was so annoyed that he almost lost his balance.

His left hand was an ice talon in the crack just above his head; it slipped, and a knee tremor shook his lower body, so that the right foot almost went. He exerted all his power of concentration to control the shaking. He held his balance. Just.

He examined the stone above his head. Right hand should have taken part of the body weight for long enough and given leverage for the long leg movement on to another of those tiny blips like the one his right foot rested on now. Then fairly easy holds and up to the top. A large whisky, a laugh at his luck and back to Sheffield. Jerry blinked as snow fell into his upturned face. There was no way up.

It couldn't be done. He needed another foot of height — eighteen inches, more like — to get his right foot on to the next hold. He looked at his left foot and saw that it was covered in fine snow. Bigger flakes began to fall.

The Peak was experiencing almost the complete range of English weather in one day.

Jerry turned, looked up again, and the small weight of the rucksack tugged at his shoulders. It came to him at that moment that he might have a chance.

If only he could balance like some bloody circus performer — for even a few seconds! Simply getting the frozen rucksack off his back with one hand was enough for the moment. As for getting the bloody beer cans into position beneath his left foot — well, that was best not thought of. Even then, they might not give him the extra height he must have.

'They've got to!' Jerry muttered to the rock face.

He wriggled with his shoulders and arms until the rucksack was hanging over his right shoulder. The beer cans clanked. How tall were they? Seven inches? Eight? Enough height, but it would take the talents of the Sheffield Monkey Man to be sure of getting them just right! He worked the stiff leather straps free and reached for one of the cold tins. *Long Life* it said on the label.

He had to catch the can between the good ledge on which his left boot rested, and his leg; hold it in position, and locate the other beer can. Then that had to go on top of the other. It wasn't possible, he told himself.

The other can was lodged below the spare sweater and the Hovis loaf. It came free and he let the rucksack drop into the space below him, not watching it vanish into the swirling blizzard. He screwed his nerves to give maximum concentration. There would only be one chance. If he failed, Hagthorpe's cemetery would know another moving little ceremony, with Andy and Anne sobbing at the graveside and going back to Sheffield to swill beer until they forgot him, and maybe Debbie there too if she wasn't busy with her trawlerman. The Pakistani landlord whose name he could never remember would chuck out the stack of indecipherable notes that were all he had to show for three years' work on his thesis. *Long Life! Exit Jerry Howard in a late-April blizzard!*

With infinite care he lowered the can, arcing his body outwards to give the greatest leverage to his feet. Snowflakes made a dancing stream of white light between his body and the slippery rock face. Then the can was quivering against its mate, two ice-cold cans of beer whose contents should have been safely inside his belly by now.

And they held upright. There was plenty of room on the ledge for both his left foot and the upright cans; there must be at least another quarter of an inch to spare, he thought.

He looked once back at the blackness that was the High Peak and saw the mask of Devil's Peak smiling enigmatically through the blizzard; he moved before he completely lost his nerve. *Up!* And arms, legs, belly, bearded face against rock, all that could be brought into play did their part. And he was on the cans, left hand searching for the good wide crack above, right hand on a sliver of rock that the yob hadn't smashed away, right foot up and over the glassy expanse above the orange slice and on to a real ledge!

Five minutes later, Jerry was on the top of Toller Edge in six inches of snow, completely exhausted.

'Never again!' he whispered. 'Never again!'

He lay for nearly ten minutes, slowly

freezing and enjoying it. He realised that he was slightly delirious. He looked at his watch, saw that there were two hours of daylight left.

He lurched to his feet, and began to trudge along the footpath that was outlined by an indentation in the snow blanket. It would take perhaps half an hour to get down off the Edge. He tried to urge himself into a loping run but abandoned the idea after twice falling perilously near the rock face. The wind bit through his anorak as if it hated him. There was nothing to be seen all about him but the gusting, billowing snow. He made a snowball and tossed it into the wind. It was thrown back, to take him on his face.

At the same moment, he tripped over an unseen chunk of rock deep below the snow and wrenched his ankle. Jerry bawled with pain above the roaring of the wind. As he went down, he caught a glimpse of the High Peak in a freak, clear moment; there was Mam Tor, bald and white. And, before it, the unpleasant black scar that the local people called Devil's Peak.

Yelling helped, so he cursed his luck, the snow, the weather forecasters who'd promised blue skies with an occasional shower later in the day, and he also cursed Professor Bruce de Matthieu for a bald-headed ponce who didn't know the difference between a good researcher and a lickspittle. It would take him an hour at this rate to get off the damned Edge. The snow was coming now in great feathery chunks that built up drifts in minutes.

'I'll lose my way,' Jerry said suddenly, aware that he had moved off the path in his pain. He limped back but his footprints had gone. And he was only halfway down the sloping ramp that led from the Edge to the Hagthorpe track. Tracks that were as familiar as the bottles on the shelf at the *Furnaceman's Arms* could lose their contours in six inches of snow. When the drifting started, the High Peak became a foreign country, its ridges, tracks, hills and valleys given an altogether outlandish appearance. Jerry knew he was lost.

After leaping like a gazelle up Toller Edge, to be overcome by fatigue in a blizzard — no! Only fools did that! Or innocents like the two Boy Scouts last year and the clot of an Army Lieutenant two years earlier. He put on a spurt and howled with pain as he did so. And he had no food, nothing! Chocolate, cheese, Hovis — all down in a two-foot deep drift of snow at the bottom of Toller Edge with the spare sweater and the compass and map.

He hobbled on in the blizzard, silent now. There was a grimness about the wind, a cold certainty about the whiteness. How had they felt, the poor young lads last year when they'd wandered on to the black crags of Devil's Peak? Cockily assertive, until they realised that after all they hadn't been prepared? Like me, Jerry thought; *and their bodies were never found!*

The grinding pain in his ankle kept him aware of his surroundings. He had to walk in a lopsided manner down the path he had found. It wasn't the right path, but it led down, and that was the important thing: to be off the heights, where the wind was an Arctic killer.

13

Where the sheep went, into the sheltered chimneys and corners — that's where he would go. And rest.

An hour later, he lay down without realising that he had done so. Actually a delirium had claimed him, one in which he thought himself opposite Janice, she of the disastrous marriages, huge bosom and hauteur at the *Furnaceman's*. She'd got a drink called a Snowball, and he had gin and Italian vermouth, iced. The ice was very cold. He opened his mouth to suck on it. He didn't realise that he was face down on a slab of stone, Darkness came, but he was not aware of it.

In another hour or two, he would have been quite cold, and some time in the night his corpse would have solidified. It was the thrumming of the Diesel engine that brought him to a last flickering of consciousness. The noise was the background murmur of the crowd in the pub; Janice told him to pay no attention, they were a set of creeps and why didn't he have another drink, on her this time because his grant hadn't come through yet.

He opened his eyes and saw the frozen rock he had rested against. 'Oh, Jesus!' he whispered.

And so he heard the noise for what it was and realised that he might, just, save himself. He crawled towards the heavy throbbing noise, careless of falling now, too scared of freezing to worry overmuch about suddenly pitching into emptiness as his rucksack had done a couple of hundred years before. Terror urged him on. The heavy beat of the engine was near, very near. But it was so dark!

Not a glimmer of light! Just the glare of the snow on the ground, and the thick curtain of whirling snow all around, still driven by a howling gale! He moved on, slowly. And there was a light.

It was a dim corona, seen through snow, but it was like some vast dawning of religious inspiration to Jerry. He pitched into the snowdrift and clawed on unconcerned.

He burst through to the roadside at a point where it ran between a cutting in the rock. He was about ten feet above the level of the road. Up against the drift from which he emerged was the source of both noise and light. It was an enormous red tanker, though Jerry was not aware of this yet.

He saw a window with a light inside. He brushed snow from his face and peered inside. Jerry saw the two writhing figures of a man and a girl. He could see the bare narrow shoulder blades of the girl and her ridged back. Despite his low physical state, he registered the mark at the base of the girl's spine: it was a red cicatrice, raised and wealed. To Jerry's delirious mind it seemed that a small red animal crawled over her. At another time he would have turned away without acknowledging what he saw, but not this time: he tapped on the window with an apologetic despair.

The couple on the seats within did not hear him at first, so he tapped again. He tried not to smile or to shriek either. The woman looked up — an attractive girl about eighteen, registered Jerry. He wondered if he would lose any fingers. The man looked out too. Both shouted something. Jerry knew he was not welcome.

The man shrugged the girl off. She began making vulgar signs at him, shouting at the same time; Jerry couldn't hear a word. Then she looked for her clothing. The driver rummaged for something, his red face suffused with anger. He wasn't going? *He couldn't!*

'Help!' screamed Jerry. 'Please! I'm hurt!'

The girl began to shout back. Then she adjusted her skirt and looked out at him. Her friend was fumbling with his clothes also. She took the opportunity of abusing Jerry directly. Winding down the window she yelled:

'Get off, you dirty peeper!' in a South Yorkshire voice.

'Please!' Jerry begged, as the driver called out to let be and shut up. 'I'm hurt! Hurt! A climber! I am! Look at my hands!'

He showed them to her in the attitude of prayer as the big Diesel engine roared back at the wind.

'Please!'

2

The big Diesel engine hammered and ground away, pushing back into the cab the smell of burning oil and such a flood of warmth that Jerry groaned aloud halfway between pleasure at being alive and pain at his dead-white nose and fingers. The girl looked sullenly at him, deeply resentful. Jerry surfaced out of his delirium.

'Give him the coffee now, lass,' the driver told her. 'Under the seat by you.' His eyes were on the swirling whiteness where the foglights punched yellow holes to the grey wall at the roadside. 'Go on!' he said again.

She didn't answer, but she did rummage under the seat. Jerry was aware of her hostility; it was the driver who had saved him.

'Here,' she muttered, slopping the smoking coffee into a cup. 'Don't spill it on me coat! It's suede!'

'Brenda's a hard-faced cow,' the driver said.

Brenda swore at him.

Jerry had met the sort before, though not one so hard so young. He was fairly sure that she would have left him to die in the snow, given a choice. The driver, whose name he didn't know yet, had hesitated. He was a big, muscular, middle-aged man with a comfortable look about him; there'd be a family, Jerry thought. Obviously he'd weighed up Jerry's condition against the situation in which he'd been caught. And either his basic humanity, or his fears of an investigation should Jerry be left, had won. He would know that the tanker's presence would have been noted by someone. Jerry preferred to think that he'd done the right thing by instinct.

His fingers had almost no feeling in them, but he could hold the mug of coffee steadily enough. The trouble was that the steam was causing his nose an exquisite agony; through tear-filled eyes, he could see the girl's hands. One was tattooed on each finger: L-O-V-E, the

19

four fingers spelt. What was on the other? He couldn't see. It seemed incredible to him that he was alive and warm, that the bitter snow was outside and he within. He remembered vaguely that he had tried to cuddle against her thin body: and she hadn't liked it. The hell with the miserable bitch; and her fingers.

'What were you doing out there anyway?' asked the driver, as they swept around a series of sharp bends,

'Walking,' said Jerry. 'It was fine when I set out.'

'What's your name, then?'

'Howard. Jerry Howard.'

'I'm Bill Ainsley. You've met Brenda.'

'Hello,' said Jerry suffused with gratitude.

'How're your hands?' asked Bill. 'I were Army in the war. I've seen frostbite. You haven't got it.'

'My hands must have been underneath. They're all right. My nose hurts.'

'Your nose wouldn't get frostbitten. They never do.'

Brenda watched each man, turning from one to another like an umpire. She

20

had a thin pink suede coat over a tiny pink skirt. Long black tights ran down to red woollen socks and heavy boots. Like all the others, she had a duffel bag stuffed to the top. And that was all.

'Wrenched your ankle too?'

'I fell over. I got stuck climbing.'

'Climbing! Climbing bloody what?' exclaimed Brenda in her pit-village voice.

'A rock face,' Jerry told her. 'Toller Edge.'

'What for? You must be mad!'

'There was two killed climbing near Capel Curig when I went through last Easter,' said Bill. 'Came off together, straight down a thousand feet.'

'Silly sods,' said Brenda.

She had dark, malevolent eyes that had been filled with a dreamy kind of fire when they had first focused on Jerry; now they were sharp and dark and hating. Bill grinned at her.

'You're lucky to have time,' he told Jerry. 'You a student?'

'Yes. That's right.'

'Students!' spat Brenda. 'They want stuffing, all of them!'

'She doesn't like students,' explained Bill. 'Two of them tried to go for her one night in the back of a Mini. She only likes lorry men.'

Brenda swore coarsely.

'Thought you were a student or a teacher,' Bill said. 'The beard.'

Brenda swore again.

Jerry saw that she was almost beautiful. Her figure wasn't ripe yet, but it would be. She was craning forward, her neck arching in a sweet curve.

'Aye, wheer you're going?' Brenda shouted. 'This isn't the Manchester road!'

'No,' explained Bill. 'I can't turn the tanker till we get to the end of this one — there isn't a place to turn for miles.'

'Then wheer are you going?'

Jerry was interested by this time; so far, he had been concerned with only the fact of his survival, the pain of sensation returning to his body, and the strange dislike of the girl.

'I could maybe get a lift back to Sheffield,' Jerry said, hearing the crunching of the massive eight tyres on drifted snow. 'A bus maybe.'

'No chance,' Bill said. 'No driver's going to turn out tonight.'

'Wheer are we going!' Brenda spat insistently.

'The caff. Castle Caff.'

'*That* dump!'

'I can turn in their yard. Get back on to the road.'

Jerry knew this place. It served as a halting-place for the men who drove the vast lorries over the backbone Of England through lanes which had been laid down for carts; the caff was useful to the walkers and campers too, though they were tolerated rather than encouraged.

'I'm not going theer!' the girl shouted.

'Then you'll have to get out and walk, lass.'

'Oh, you sod.'

'And sod you,' said Bill equably. The huge tanker skidded for seconds on locked wheels as he took it round a steep curve. Jerry looked out and saw a glimpse of lights far below in a break in the blizzard. They were climbing now along the shoulder of the rock he had seen from the gritstone edge: they would climb

23

further until they were halfway up the shivering, loose shale face of Devil's Peak, right up to the curious projection of rocks that from a distance, and in the right light, had the configuration of a pair of curved horns. All the local peaks had names — Mam Tor and Chee Tor and Mam Nick — usually the ancient names of forgotten peoples. None was so appropriately named as this. It seemed strange, almost ironical, to be sitting in a tanker after almost freezing to death and then making for Devil's Peak which had seemed to leer at him only an hour or two ago. But he wanted to go back to Sheffield. It was Friday, and Friday night was beer and darts night.

'Maybe there'll be a lorry at the caff,' he said. 'You know, Bill, going back my way.'

'Could be,' Bill agreed. 'Still, you're out of trouble, aren't you?'

He looked worried. The unspoken question was in the air. Would Jerry make any comment on the presence of the girl? Jerry sensed the man's discomfort.

'Why not leave me at the caff?' he said.

'You go on — if I can't get a lift, I'll stay till morning.'

Bill grinned suddenly, his fleshy face relaxed completely, 'Aye. Brenda and me'll go on to Manchester. Sure you'll be all right?'

Jerry checked on the condition of his fingers, nose and toes. All seemed to be functioning normally, though there was still a feeling of a tightening and painful expansion of the extremities of his body.

'Don't worry about me.'

Brenda looked at him: 'Who's worrying?'

'Cow,' said Bill pleasantly. 'Soon be at the caff. Can't stay long, though. The drifts are getting up. There won't be many more trucks going through after me. Not tonight.'

The girl was pressed against Jerry's body, but there was little heat to be gained from her; it was as though she could insulate herself from him. He began to worry, for he was normally attractive to women; however partisan the lorry girls might be, this one was hostile in an unusual way. So she'd been messed about

25

by a couple of drunk undergraduates. So what? He found himself angry in return.

'Theer,' said the girl suddenly. There were lights beside the road a few yards ahead. The tanker was moving cautiously up the narrow road so that when she spotted the caff Bill could turn in easily.

'Let me buy you a drink. A meal or something,' Jerry said, as the vast engine was quiet. 'Bill. And you, Brenda.'

Brenda pushed past him contemptuously. She said nothing as she jumped into the howling night.

'A cup of tea then,' said Bill. 'You all right to get out?'

Jerry remembered how he had been hauled in by the man, a limp and frozen bundle desperate for warmth.

'I'm all right,' he said.

They got down, Bill jumping lightly, Jerry lowering himself tortuously on to his sore ankle. Bill waited for him in the whipping shock of the wind and snow.

He shouted something above the wind. 'She's a cow . . . always on the hills . . . still, she's company on the run!'

The caff was a single-storied building

roofed in white-grey concrete panels that sloped away to take the edge off the prevailing wind. The rest of the building was much older — it was built massively from blocks of the local gritstone, green and weathered from exposure to years of howling gales. In the junction of two pinnacles of rock where the caff was built, the wind boiled up the snow so that it danced as if in a tornado's grip. Snow had drifted to the side of the building nearest the tanker to a depth of three feet, up to the windows. It was an odd place to find a caff, but it seemed to suit the couple who ran it. It did a fair business. Not tonight, however. There wasn't another lorry or car in the big park.

Jerry hobbled his way to the door and pushed inside.

Brenda was already drinking. She was in the act of lighting a cigarette when they came in.

'Shut door quick!' she yelled. 'It's bloody frozen! And I'm not staying here long either!'

Raybould himself was at the counter, hidden from view by a large coffee urn except for the top of his bald head which shone damply in the white neon lighting. He emerged as he heard the door slam shut.

'Hello, Bill!' he called. 'You look like Father Christmas — and you look perished,' he added to Jerry.

'I got stuck walking,' said Jerry. 'I can't get back to Sheffield — '

'That you can't! Road's blocked t'other side of Hathersage! Just got it from Radio Sheffield!'

'Found him near frozen,' said Bill. 'He'd been up Toller Edge.'

Jerry didn't want a discussion of his encounter with near-death. He shivered, the hot delirium he had felt in the cab returning once more.

'So have you a bed for the night?' he stuttered.

'Aye! You as well, Bill?'

'No. Brenda and me's pushing on.'

'I wouldn't,' Raybould said. He was glancing from Bill to Brenda with a wet excitement in his slightly bulbous blue eyes. Jerry could see his nose twitching, as if he were on a strong scent. His features were small, clustered in the middle of his face — eyes, nose, mouth, all scrunched together, alert like a stoat's.

Brenda saw the look he gave her and snorted. She took her tea across to the big coal fire that blazed furiously into the brick chimney; she sat on a low chair beside a big brass coal-scuttle that Jerry didn't recall seeing before. But it had been summer then, so perhaps it had been out of sight; there was no call for such a fire when the High Peak was warm and friendly. The two men, Raybould and Bill, talked about the state of the roads to Manchester; Bill was confident that his big red tanker would get through. He wouldn't stop to put on chains, just for a cup of tea. And he wouldn't let Jerry pay after all.

'No need for that, lad,' Bill said. 'I was glad to help. Doesn't need paying for. How's the ankle?'

'Fall, did you?' called Raybould. 'We get a lot of broken legs. Those buggers who do the climbing. You'd think they'd know what they were about, what with ropes and helmets and that. But they're

29

always falling off. We buried one over Christmas.'

Jerry's heart lurched. He was back on the face momentarily, sick with the realisation that the rock jug had been knocked off and that he'd committed himself to going up. He saw Brenda's thin smile. She had ungenerous but pretty red lips turned both up and down in an expression that was between a snarl and a look of amusement: Then she turned away and began tracing the pattern along the edge of the brass scuttle.

Jerry fought against the flood of delirium that threatened to overcome his senses. He unlaced his boots, controlling his shaking hands only with difficulty. He inspected his ankle. There was a soggy feel about the tendons on the outside as if the swelling had just started.

'I'll be all right in a day or two,' he told Bill. Raybould noticed his condition at last.

'Best get yourself dry!' he said. 'Brenda, come away from in front of the fire. Put your jacket over the chair. Come on Brenda!'

But she wasn't listening. Jerry could see her caressing the brass fire-bucket with gentle lascivious movements. T-R-U-E he spelt out on the fingers of her left hand. The long, thin fingers were tracing hypnotic patterns in the firelight; the metal was red and brassily yellow. She stared down, quite intent on her game. Jerry saw Raybould's face set in an expression of unequivocal lust; in the summer he tried to chat up the girl-walkers, though not when his wife was about. It was their long brown legs that fascinated him. Jerry's senses began to swim away from him as the glittering brass and the heat and the girl's insidious movements hypnotised him. He heard the conversation as if through a series of transparent curtains, faintly, distantly.

'Come on, Brenda,' ordered Bill Ainsley. 'We'll get off now.'

Still she didn't look up.

'That bloody brass tub!' said Raybould. 'She always sits over it! *Brenda!*'

'Wrap up! Get off!' she added, as something white and angry rushed towards her. 'Bloody pest!'

Jerry's eyes had begun to close. He blinked awake as he heard a faint yipping sound: *Yip-yip-yip! Yap! Yip-yip!* He looked at his feet and saw a white blur, red mouth open, white fragile teeth bared: it was — *a chicken?* A chicken! Yipping at the lorry-girl, who glowered back at it, snarling her own vicious answer. Jerry shuddered. The chicken had little curls all over its body. *Yip-yip!* it went. *Yip-yip-yip!*

'Not a barking chicken!' he said in anguish. 'There isn't such a thing.'

'A barking what!' Bill said. 'Lad, you're bad!'

'Come out, Sukie!' Raybould said, and Jerry realised that he was looking at a frightened and angry white miniature poodle, all thin bones and fluff. 'Leave her alone, Sukie!'

The poodle backed off and went to the door leading to the kitchen.

'Barking chicken!' laughed Bill Ainsley. 'Coming, lass?' he asked Brenda.

'You could stay,' Raybould offered.

'Oh no she couldn't!' called a woman from the doorway at the back of the counter. 'I don't want her sort here. Sukie! Go back!' she ordered the poodle.

It was Raybould's wife, a tall, thin woman of about fifty; she looked at her husband, daring him to repeat his invitation. Brenda stared at the woman. Jerry saw a strange expression in her eyes again, that dreamy, unfocused emptiness he had first seen when he was in a half-conscious state himself. She touched the brass bucket again with her tattooed hands, once, twice. Then she grinned at Bill as any teenager might, jumped to her feet and slouched to the door. Mrs. Raybould watched carefully. Sukie yipped twice in triumph.

'So you're all right?' Bill asked Jerry.

'No need to worry,' Jerry said. 'I'm fine. If you hadn't got out — '

'Aye, well,' Bill said. 'No harm done.'

'If you ever get to the *Furnaceman's* in Sheffield — Townsend Street — I'd like to buy you a drink.'

'Aye. All right, lad.'

He called his goodnights and ushered Brenda out into the blizzard. Jerry knew he had been lucky. He sat close to the fire and saw his sweater and anorak begin to steam.

Mrs. Raybould crossed to him:

'Why, you're wet through! You're shaking! Sam, get him a blanket! He'll have to dry off! How about something to eat, if you're staying? You are, aren't you? Well, you'll have to. There won't be any going back to Sheffield, not tonight. And if that A57 stays open Manchester way, it'll be a miracle! Now, Sam!'

Raybould went for the blanket.

'Bacon and sausage?' Mrs. Raybould said. 'You've been in here before, haven't you?' She petted the little poodle bitch, which sniffed at Jerry.

'A few times.'

'You were with some climbers.'

'That's right,' Jerry said. The bitch inspected his ankle. Mrs. Raybould did not object. Jerry was suddenly violently hungry. 'I could do with that bacon and sausage. And some eggs.'

'Tea and bread and butter,' Mrs. Raybould decided. 'You had a girl with you.'

'Yes,' said Jerry. The woman hadn't

34

been anything like so agreeable when he and Deborah had called in for a meal one day in August. The food was stale, warmed up probably.

'Those lorry girls,' Mrs. Raybould grumbled. 'Come in and sit all night with a cup of tea. Especially her. *He* doesn't mind. Sukie hates her! Hurry up, Sam!' she called. 'I'll get your meal.'

Jerry leaned forward towards the coal fire and saw what the girl had been entranced by. Around the rim of the coalscuttle was a row of figures. They seemed to dance in the yellow and red flames. Raybould came up behind him.

'Here's a blanket — get your things off.' Jerry closed his eyes, swaying with drowsiness. He had been near death and he was drunk with heat. 'You're a teacher, aren't you?' Raybould asked.

Jerry managed to get the soaking tee-shirt off. Then the corduroy trousers. He felt the rough army blanket on his skin.

'Just out by yourself, then?'

'That's it.'

Jerry didn't want questions about his

escape from death; it was too close, too real. He pointed to the figures:

'I haven't seen this before.'

'The old scuttle fell to bits, so I use this. It's heavy to hump about.'

'The engravings are good.'

'Should be. It came from the Castle.'

Jerry blinked in the glare as a burst of blue-red flame shot up the chimney. It had been an odd sort of day, what with the blizzard coming up and the girl hating him. He was aware that he had not recovered from the effects of the climb and the gradual freezing in the drift. It was a sign of complete exhaustion when you had fantasies like thinking you were boozing at the *Furnaceman's* when you were lying face down in the snow; and thinking that Sukie was a chicken because she was white and stood on her hind legs yipping at Brenda. He talked more or less to reassure himself that he was able to:

'It's a special kind of engraving,' he said. 'Look — the figures aren't directly representational. They're faceless — that's special. And their lower limbs aren't shown in detail. It's meant to be

36

impressionistic. You're supposed to see the figures dancing in a fast step, blurred as if they were before you in poor light.'

'So you're a student?' Raybould asked. 'I mean, you talk like one. You from the University? You're a bit old, like.'

'I'm at the University.'

'Aye?'

Raybould settled himself opposite Jerry. Both men watched the engravings.

'I'm reading for a higher degree. Historical research.'

'I like a bit of history.'

'I'm doing a study of lost villages,' Jerry said, seeing Raymould's interest. He knew he shouldn't describe his work, since it was a dead bore to anyone but a few historians

'Lost villages? Who lost them?' Raybould was mildly amused. His small features moved closer together, nose to mouth, eyes almost meeting in merriment.

'They got built over, or the ruins sank into the ground during the past thousand years.'

'Aye?'

'If you map their distribution, you get a picture of England as it was in that time.'

'Oh, aye?' said Raybould, now uninterested. He gestured to the thick wall behind the open fireplace. 'This is old, you know. A bit of the old castle before it was bombed.'

Jerry's professional interest was immediately engaged.

'What castle?'

'This! Castle Caff, that's this place!'

'I know what you call it. But I didn't know it was a castle!'

No wonder Professor Bruce de Matthieu was opposed to the study he'd been working on. The fat, smarmy-voiced old bastard had been cutting just before Christmas: 'All very well writing about Lost Villages, Howard, but isn't it about time you found one or two?' And here was a bloody castle that he hadn't known about!

'Aye, well, a sort of castle,' said Raybould. 'The Nazis blew it up in the war. Bombed it, like. Blew it to buggery!'

Jerry thought he had misheard when Raybould first referred to a bombing.

Now he adjusted mentally. A castle bombed!

'What did they bomb it for?'

'Here's your sausage, bacon and eggs!' Mrs. Raybould called. 'No, stay by the fire — I'll move this table. Sam!'

Sam obliged and the scent of the food overcame Jerry. They watched him eat for a moment and then Mrs. Raybould crossed to the window.

'You couldn't see a hand in front of you!' she called. 'Telephone lines will be down. And electric. Three days, Sam?'

'About that,' Raybould said to her. He was interested in Jerry's reaction to his story. 'I don't know why they bombed it. But they did. Only this part were left. And the cellars.'

Jerry glanced down and saw the shifting, enigmatic figures in their eternal frozen dance. A medieval castle right under his nose and he hadn't known it existed! He might as well get a job now and forget the research. Something simple, like truck-driving. There were perks. Hard-faced Brenda, for one. Or maybe not.

'Is it all right?' asked Mrs. Raybould.

'The best I've ever eaten,' said Jerry truthfully. His mouth full of fried egg, he asked Raybould: 'When was the castle built?'

Raybould shrugged. 'I couldn't say.'

'It can't be medieval!'

'Oh no?' said Mrs. Raybould, She changed the subject, 'They'll never get through,' she said. '*Her* and Bill's tanker. Never! We'll have snow for three days. Be a few caught in it on the Peak.'

She didn't seem particularly unhappy or sympathetic about the prospect. But Jerry's belly was full, and his mind was drowsily filled with a mild curiosity about the caff. The building could be old, but not seven or eight hundred years old like the other crumbling relics of Henry Plantagenet's troubled reign. It was too much of an effort to ask any more questions, though. He was amazingly tired.

The door swung open, causing a huge draught that brought a surly belch of flame and smoke into the room. Jerry looked round bewildered and saw the snow-covered slight figure trying to shut the door.

'Oh no,' said Mrs. Raybould.

'Well wheer else could we come!' Brenda yelled. 'He's stuck in a sodding drift miles down the Hagthorpe road. I came on. I weren't staying to freeze out there!'

She made for the fire and stood with the snow turning to big drops of water that fell on to Jerry's bare feet.

'She'll have to stay,' said Sam Raybould.

Mrs. Raybould glared and collected the dirty plates. Sam Raybould's watery eyes were on the girl's flushed face. There was an intent, feral look on his face.

'I'll get off to bed, if you don't mind, Mrs. Raybould,' Jerry said. He hated confrontations, which was why Debbie had gone. She had said as much. Often. He was an intellectual, which meant that when he had to make decisions on ordinary everyday matters like rows, marriage, money, and where to live, he got confused. Debbie didn't admire this trait. He knew it but refused to admit it to himself; when there were difficulties, he evaded them. She was a girl who took life head on. 'All right, Mrs. Raybould?'

She led the way, silently loathing the lorry-girl.

3

Jerry's dreams were bad. He woke up sweating to see a ghostly white radiance from the lightly-curtained window; there was a harsh scratching on the glass, and it took him a few seconds to realise that it was frozen snow. Three more beds in the bleak, cold room added a certain atmosphere of desolation, so that he was filled with a peculiar sense of aloneness. At once, he thought of the lorry-girl. Brenda. Then he was worried. He had not visualised Debbie Hutchinson. Was she already a completed experience?

He had dreamt of Brenda, or at least she had been in the dream. Her hands had writhed over the coal bucket making a pattern of blue and white tattoos. The words were no longer the pathetic invocation to Eros. T-R-U-E L-O-V-E had given way to a cabalistic sign made up of fire and frozen white fingers. And the barking chicken was gnawing something, worrying

43

it with greedy fangs. *Sukie — sucky — Sukie!* someone was yelling. *We want you, Sukie!* And there was a red thing. Half-rat, half-toad, that jumped from Brenda's hands that weren't hands any more, but living and horrible entities of their own; and the red thing was crawling not on the scrawny lorry-girl's back but on his own, so that Jerry woke up repressing a convulsive yell of terror. He shuddered, body warm, but full of a cold dread. It was still night, he sensed. There were hours yet of the glaring night.

Debbie came back to him, Debbie who was plump and jam-packed with life. He centred his thoughts about her, trying to get rid of the dread that had gripped him. He couldn't. The girl's hating eyes, dark brown like thick smoke, haunted him. He dived under the hot bedclothes and tried to sleep, muffling the scratching of the driven snow and comforting his exhausted body with the bed's warmth. Yet the dream couldn't be driven away. It settled on him like a giant crow.

Jerry pushed the clothes back again, annoyed and fearful. He saw a huge shape bending over him. Primitive terror reinforced the hallucinated state left over from his dream. And he couldn't yell now.

'They were right,' came Bill Ainsley's everyday voice. 'The Manchester road's blocked solid. Did I wake you?'

Jerry gulped and cursed himself for a fool once more; he had succumbed. like a teenager at a demo, to hysteria. There was nothing that the mind should fear; so why tremble at the memory of a dream?

'I turned and pressed on my bad ankle,' said Jerry. 'What time is it?'

'Half past one. I've been securing the rig. So it won't slip if the drift melts. I reckon there's been a bit of a landslip. You all right, lad?'

'Jerry.'

'Jerry then. No more barking chickens!'

'No.' But there had been the dream. 'I was sweating.'

'Aye, you would. You get that with exposure,' Bill said, taking off his coat. 'Sam and Sylvia told me to keep quiet. Want to get back to sleep?'

'Yes. I reckon I could sleep now.'

'Aye. You'll get plenty of time for sleep.

The Rayboulds reckon we'll be here three days.'

'Three days?'

'About that. They won't bother open-ing up this side road. It'll just drift full again in a few hours. And I bet they'll find half the road's gone! Still, I've been in worse places.'

Bill shivered as he lowered his big body into the cold bed. He was asleep before Jerry, but Jerry could listen to the snow and not grow cold in the pit of the belly; sleep came, and, blessedly, no more of the writhing, haunted dreams.

Next morning, both men were awak-ened by the Rayboulds quarrelling. The wind still rattled at the windows, the snow still rapped on the glass, but above the noise they could hear the high-pitched voice of Mrs. Raybould and the yelps of her husband. The words were muffled by the thick old walls, but their intent was clear from the odd distinguishable word: *Brenda.*

Bill lit a cigarette and passed the packet. Jerry refused and began to wheeze with a bronchial cough, so that for a while he lost the progress of the row. By the time he had recovered his breath, the voices were at a distance, but they were still angry, still full of expostulation on Raybould's part and furious contempt on his wife's.

'Stuck here for three days,' Bill Ainsley said: 'She's trouble, that lass. Always was. But what can you do? You get lonely on the road all day and night. I mean, why not, when it's laid on?'

'Why not?' agreed Jerry. His night curiosity about the girl returned. 'She always sticks to this part of the country?' he asked.

Bill slid out of bed and drew on his trousers.

'Between Sheffield and Manchester, that's where you'll find her. North a bit too, out as far as Carlisle sometimes in the summer, but she doesn't go far from the hills.'

'And she's trouble?'

Bill shrugged. 'She's better looking than most of the old slags. So there's sometimes a fight. But I wasn't thinking of that.'

'Oh?'

Bill had finished dressing. 'No.'

Mrs. Raybould's voice broke through from near the bedroom door, this time in an exasperated series of instructions to Raybould, concerned with shutters, coal, bacon and the poodle bitch. It was obvious who was the authority in the Castle Café.

'So what trouble?' Jerry asked, but Bill was not forthcoming. The big driver hadn't the wit to turn the conversation, so he said nothing at all. An old traveller, he had a razor with him. Ignoring Jerry's question, he got on with his toilet, but his attitude did not suggest hostility. It was irritating, but Jerry recognised the York-shireman's decision as final. Simply, he wouldn't talk about the girl. When he had finished, he turned to Jerry: 'You'll not be wanting this?'

'I only grew it to look older,' Jerry said. 'When I was a student first, years ago.'

'Aye?'

'You think we'll be here three days?'

'Sure on it. I rang through to our depot last night. They reckon on drifts up to twelve foot on the Peak roads. Then the lines were down, and I couldn't get through later on. But the forecast was bad on the radio too. Look for yourself.'

Jerry looked out of the window. There was little to see, except for the white sheeting of flying frozen snowflakes and, occasionally, a glimpse of the cold expanse beyond. The café was in an Arctic world now, cut off from the comfortable civilisation on each side of the Pennines. Down in Sheffield, there would be bulletins about the state of the roads, and a surprised and pleased pride about the English weather; burst pipes would count for nothing against the pleasure of proving the forecasters wrong. Jerry looked again and, to his right, saw the imposing mass of Devil's Peak rising sheer into the whiteness. One of the natural rock features from which the Peak took its name was glistening, frosted over with the phenomenon of verglass: impacted water crystals under pressure. But the rock was harsh and black underneath. How, he thought, was he to spend three days in this wilderness?

Then he remembered the intriguing question of the castle's origins. He decided to ask Raybould about them, that was, when he'd recovered from his wife's assaults. The place couldn't be medieval! It wasn't shown on any map of the Peak, not any he'd seen.

'That's bacon,' said Bill Ainsley, sniffing the smell from the kitchen. 'I hope they've got plenty laid in.'

'They'd have enough for weeks,' Jerry said.

'Aye, for us. But there'll be others along. We'll not be the only silly buggers to be caught on the roads, you watch. Eat what you can while you can! Ready?'

Bill slicked his thinning hair to his satisfaction. Jerry ran a hand through his own wiry hair and sluiced cold water over his face. He still ached, and the ankle pulled sickeningly when he forgot to lean his weight on his good foot.

'Ready,' he said, envying Bill his acceptance of life.

Brenda was already eating. Raybould watched her covertly from the counter, which he was wiping down with a greasy cloth. She wore the same slight dress, revealing thin, shapely legs and an expanse of muscular thigh; to Jerry, she seemed ridiculously young, like the first-year girls coming up full of zest, stuffed to the gills with A levels lore and anxious to shed their inhibitions. He tried to find a word for her and failed. *Shifty?* She wasn't that. There was an assuredness about her. *Vulnerable?* No. She was almost smug in her contempt of others. *Promiscuous?* Certainly, if her activity with Bill in the cab was any guide. But she was more. He couldn't find the word for her. But there was one.

She ate with one hand, whilst the other reached out for the brass coal-scuttle. In the smoky firelight she let her hands flutter about the eerie figures. Jerry swallowed hard, remembering the sweaty terrors of the night

'It's ready,' Raybould called. 'I've given Brenda hers. Had enough bacon, love? More toast?'

'No,' she said. 'I'll have some tea.' She surveyed Bill for a moment. 'How long?'

Bill grinned at her. 'Like Sam said last

51

night. There'll be no leaving for days.'

'Days!'

Her gaze took in the low, stone-walled room. Jerry followed her look. Ten tables, each with an assortment of chairs, plastic-topped, with a complement of H.P. sauce and salt; three windows, one cracked at the top but papered over with brown tape; a bench by the large door covered in old comics and magazines; a pin-table with a notice 'Out of Order' which Jerry had seen months before. A cigarette machine with no cigarettes. Two books on the window sill. Jerry was glad to see them.

'What am I going to do here for days? *Days!*'

Mrs. Raybould with Sukie at her heels came in to hear her question.

'There'd better not be any messing about in my café!' she said. 'Oh, no! I've heard — I always said it was you that got that Army lad in trouble.'

Now the girl's more or less amused contempt turned to something quite different. She placed the cleaned plate down on a table and got to her feet; Jerry noticed her hand still trailing on the coalscuttle.

'You what!'

The poodle bitch yipped at her feebly.

'Now, Sylvia!' warned Sam. 'No call for that! She said at the time she'd seen him, that was all.'

Jerry was fascinated by the girl's eyes. They had the dark, hating quality with which they had regarded him through the window of the cab, but something more now. There was a cruel fire in them, something like that at the centre of the uncertain coal fire: a quality of latent energy needing only a wind of anger to bring it out in a red glow.

'I didn't!' came the uncouth, menacing tones from the pretty mouth. 'I didn't and anyone says so is a liar! I saw him and he asked where were t'Ole and I told him!'

Mrs. Raybould was herself possessed by a fierce anger.

'Then why didn't you tell him bad weather were coming! You knew — he'd never seen the mists coming up like they do! You had! You're always looking for trouble, aren't you! By God, girl, if it weren't for the snow, I'd see you on your way now!'

The girl smiled at her, concealing the red rage in her fire-dark eyes.

'Well you can't, can you? Here for days, that's what we are.' She looked at Raybould. The man was acutely uncomfortable, a prey to middle-aged sexual fantasies. And the girl knew it. 'I'll have to make myself useful, won't I?' she asked slyly.

'Watch it.' warned Bill easily.

Jerry wanted to know more. It wasn't the time to ask, however. He had a dozen questions to ask, but the slightly farcical scenes he watched enabled him to subdue them.

'Somebody say breakfast?' he asked.

The girl sat down and searched in her duffel bag for a cigarette. Bill ignored her, and gradually Mrs. Raybould turned away from the girl and the fireplace. Her gaze rested on Jerry.

'Dropouts!' she snorted, 'Students!'

When the bacon came, Jerry's portion was greasily underdone.

Afterwards, Raybould cleared the pots

away and came across to the two men.

'Goes on a bit,' he offered. 'The wife. She never wanted this place, and she'd give it away if she had her way. I don't mind it. It's very healthy, what with the wind. She doesn't take to the young birds, though.'

'Mine doesn't,' Bill said in sympathy.

'Mine's left me,' Jerry said as the two men looked at him. 'Gone back home. Another bloke.'

'Ah, well, you're all like that these days, aren't you?' Raybould answered, taking the opportunity of looking at Brenda. 'I mean, you don't bother marrying, do you?'

'I hadn't thought about it,' said Jerry, realising that it was the truth. 'You don't when you're still a student.'

'Can't be a student all your life,' Bill said.

'I wish I'd been one,' Raybould said.

Mrs. Raybould looked in. She went away, saying nothing, Sukie trotting at her heels. Brenda dozed by the fire, content to let her fingers trail over the brass figures. Noticing her, Jerry was all curiosity. If he couldn't ask Bill questions about her, at least he could ask Raybould about the café.

'You were talking about the place being bombed,' he said. 'You're not joking? I mean, who'd want to bomb an old castle?'

Raybould was glad to have a hearer. 'Let me get the old newspapers,' he said, 'I had them sent out when we put a roof on the place in '47. The back issues, like.'

Jerry approved. Contemporary documents, that was the thing. But whilst Raybould was away in the café's living-quarters, Bill told most of it. Bill Ainsley knew the Peak stories.

'It was a big four-engined job that strayed out here after bombing Hull. They'd got a few bombs left, so they were looking for somewhere handy to unload them — no opposition much at night. The pilot strayed out here. He knew he was in trouble so he jettisoned the bombs. Smack bang on the castle. Killed a few sheep, that was all. The place had been derelict for years.'

Brenda was listening. Her dark eyes were on Bill.

'Funny thing,' Bill went on. The pilot said he'd been shot at.

'Why is that funny?' asked Jerry.

'He must have been mistaken. There'd not be guns this far west. There'd be batteries protecting Sheffield, but nothing here.'

Raybould came back with a blue manilla folder.

'It's all there,' he said. 'Pictures and all. And the Heinkel that did the damage!'

Brenda came across too. The old, yellowing newsprint was like something from prehistory, on the wings of the Heinkel the crosses resembled grave-markers; and they were. The plane was smashed on a hillside like a big moth under a boy's cruel foot. Jerry felt Brenda's body brush coldly against him. For no reason at all he thought of the eerie dream; and of the red mark at the base of her spine as she writhed on big Bill Ainsley. She went away after looking at the pictures.

NAZIS DESTROY HISTORIC CASTLE, the headlines said. DEVIL'S PEAK LANDSLIDE KILLS FOUR SHEEP.

Jerry read through the lengthy piece

quickly. The only survivor of the crash was the pilot, a youth from Hamburg who had complained bitterly of being shot out of the sky by a new kind of weapon; dying from multiple injuries aggravated by rage, he had spoken of a green fire that twisted his plane about the sky until it was forced down into the sides of Devil's Peak, causing a landslip and the deaths of his crew, to say nothing of the loss of four valuable sheep. The Earl of Brindley's eighteenth-century castle was the main casualty, however.

'There,' said Jerry triumphantly. 'I knew it couldn't be medieval.'

'What?' asked Raybould, looking again at the plane.

'The Castle! It must be some kind of folly — a Gothic folly. The period's right — eighteenth century.'

Bill smiled at his enthusiasm as he went to the walls and tapped them with a bottle of H.P. sauce. Raybould was somewhat piqued, an expert not consulted.

'Well, it's old,' he muttered. 'And the cellars.'

Jerry returned to the papers.

'April the 30th,' he read. 'About this time of the year. I wonder what they thought of England when they were coming down?'

'I'd my fill of them,' said Bill Ainsley, 'In the Army.'

'And me,' said Raybould. 'I was Catering Corps.'

Jerry had the scholar's excitement.

'Who was this Brindley character?' he asked Raybould. 'Can't say I've heard of him. My period's earlier than that.'

He had forgotten all he ever knew of events after about 1490. Up to then, life was real, full of wars and kings, charters and chancellors, teaure systems and mints. It struck him that he could be called narrow-minded.

Raybould collected his news cuttings, still slightly offended.

'He was a bad 'un. Built this place for his mates. Not this here,' he said, pointing to the massive stone walls. 'This was just part of the outbuildings, storerooms probably. They 'dozed the ruins flat. Where the lorries park. I mean the Castle.

He had some funny ideas.'

Jerry groped at memories and cursed his lack of general knowledge. Brenda was smiling at him as if she could help; but she looked away, down at the coalscuttle.

'Funny ideas?'

'Nasty,' said Raybould. 'Why d'you think they call the place Devil's Peak?'

4

It was too much for Jerry. 'You're not going to tell me it's devil-mongering? Oh, no! Not black magic!'

The trouble with Derbyshire was that you got these tales. There was the legend of the Black Pig of Grendelholme, all about midnight rides by old-age pensioners who mixed belladonna draughts in the hope that they could find someone to bewitch.

The things people could bring themselves to believe! What else was there? Something here, at this tatty caff? Jerry began to laugh softly at himself. Raybould was indignant. 'Well, there was a right bad 'un lived here, I can tell you! A right bad 'un!'

Jerry began to laugh, making Raybould angry. And the girl was eyeing him with her familiar look of loathing.

'Not a crew of black magickers!'

'Aye,' said Raybould, 'there was! And

down in the caverns too — down there, Mr. Clever Bloody Student!'

'Not here!' Jerry was still dismissive.

'There was!' Raybould said dramatically, pointing to the back of the caff towards the cliff behind. 'Right there!'

Something about his watery blue eyes stopped Jerry's mirth.

Or perhaps it was the cold gaze of the girl's smoky eyes; she turned away from the two men to look at the fire. Jerry saw her tracing the strange patterns in the coalscuttle once more.

Jerry spoke in a normal voice:

'I didn't mean to be rude, Mr. Raybould. It's just that I've read a lot of medieval accounts of witchcraft, and they've always struck me as being pitiful rather than horrifying. I'm sorry.'

'Ah, well,' said Raybould. 'I don't know about that.'

Bill Ainsley had finished his perusal of yesterday's sports pages in the *Daily Mirror*. He lit another cigarette and watched Brenda for a while. Then he walked across to the broken pinball machine and tried the handle a few times.

Jerry pointed to the big old fireplace:

'So this was part of the old castle too, was it, Mr. Raybould? Anything else?'

'The cellars,' Raybould answered. Jerry could see that he was still resentful. 'The cellars was the Castle's.'

'What cellars?' asked Jerry.

Raybould grunted: 'The original cellars — them as was the Castle's.'

'And you use them?' asked Jerry.

'Yes. For coal,' said Raybould. 'And paraffin. There's some stretchers too the Rescue Service leave. Other stuff. Boxes. Ropes.' He grinned, showing unclean dentures. 'For the climbers as can't climb.'

'There's plenty of those,' said Bill Ainsley.

The driver was bored. He was an active man who wished for action. Jerry wondered if he would try to get the girl to himself; probably not, with Mrs. Raybould anxious to stamp out the girl's sexuality. Raybould's scrunched-up features were still set in an attitude of resentment, though he too was aware of the silent girl at the fireside.

Jerry tried a tactic that had stood him in good stead in tutorials:

'I always find these Derbyshire legends a drag,' he said. 'You find there's nothing but a poor old woman who's been burned because she's got a pet cat, and because she calls it Titty or something, then it's her familiar and she suckles it at the breast. So she's a witch and the villagers burn her. Or take this Black Pig business. I read a fourteenth-century dialect poem not long since. It was about the Black Pig. Someone's supposed to have been carried off into some local cavern by it and — '

''Ag 'Ole,' the girl said quietly.

Jerry was trying to rouse Raybould to a defence of his story. He went on:

'It may have been Hag Hole, Brenda, but the point is — '

'It were 'Ag 'Ole.'

Raybould responded too:

'Aye! Hag 'Ole! That's the other side of Devil's Peak. She's right, the lass is! And it's where the Brindleys went, every last one of 'em, father, son, grandfather Lord

Titus that had the beast's foot, cousins, all the bloody lot on 'em! The lot gone, just like that!'

He threw his thin arms into the air with a triumphant gesture, daring Jerry to contradict him.

'Down 'Ag Hole?' Bill Ainsley said.

'Aye!' said Raybould. 'And never seen again!'

Jerry was impressed by his performance. Raybould believed in the story. He himself could guess the source of the legend — after all, it was his job to discover the seeds of truth in unlikely tales. He determined to do so.

'What happened, Mr. Raybould?'

'The Devil took 'em!' Raybould said, but again he had gone too far. Seeing the corners of Jerry's mouth twitching he turned away. 'Bugger you!' he muttered, then he was gone behind his counter to clatter with the coffee machine.

Bill Ainsley shrugged and sat beside Brenda for a while, reading the sports pages once again. He got up from time to time, but the girl ignored him. She seemed satisfied to sit by the fire, occasionally building a piece of coal into the structure of black and red and yellow before her. Bill patted her thin, elegant knee once, but she pushed him away.

He caught Jerry's eye and looked at Raybould.

'He's in a bit of a mood,' the lorry-man said. 'Silly sod.' But it was said good-humouredly. He got to his feet. 'I'm going out to see how the rig's managing. I've got a shirt and socks I didn't bring.' He dug Brenda in the ribs. 'You coming for the walk, love?'

She looked through the window amazedly: 'In that!'

The wind pounded against the glass, and the snow whirled away over the top of the Peak towards Sheffield and the valley of the Don. Bill Ainsley looked sheepish.

'Then I'll go myself.'

Jerry decided not to approach Raybould again until he had recovered from his bout of ill temper. When the driver had gone, in a whirlwind of frozen snowflakes, he read the paper in a desultory way and examined the two paperback novels someone had left on the windowsill by the pinball machine. The first three pages were missing from the Western, and the science fiction novel was one by a maniacal Englishman whose work he did not admire. He tested his weight on the ankle, and felt the vicious jabs lancing through the nerves with the usual second day violence. It would be a week before he could walk without pain. Maybe Debbie would be back by then. He wondered what he would say to her.

He looked across at the thin-boned girl by the fire. There was a sexual awareness about her that Bill Ainsley had not been able to resist. Jerry was driven to momentary anguish at the thought of Debbie with the trawler captain; he had never seen him, not even a photograph, but there had been the long letters twice a week.

Jerry wondered if that was the attraction: was the fisherman interesting simply because he had something to say? But it didn't do any good to dwell on his own shortcomings. There was a task here that he was trained for.

'I'm a researcher,' he said crisply to Brenda. 'I'd like to hear about the Brindley legend. Now. What was he? A bit of a demonologist?'

Brenda looked and sneered.

'It's my job to find out,' Jerry said again. 'Won't you tell me what you know?' He had a moment's inspiration. 'Didn't I hear that you know something of a more recent disappearance? I mean, didn't Mrs. Raybould say you knew about that Army Lieutenant?'

Brenda stilled her thin fingers for a moment. Jerry felt a growing annoyance.

'Did you see him?'

Brenda turned to him. He read fury in the firedark eyes:

'Who says I did?'

'Mr. Raybould.'

'He can get stuffed. So can you.'

Jerry felt angry now. 'We're stuck here! Why can't we just talk?'

She swore at him.

Jerry walked away from her, too angry to trust himself near her now. Three days in this place! Stuck with a lorry-man's whore and nothing to read! And no chance of even taking a walk!

'I'd go back to bed,' said Raybould. 'There's nowt else to do when the snow comes. Get some sleep.'

He looked quickly at Brenda, and Jerry could see his mind working. Brenda was the focus of all three men's thoughts. Jerry felt a vindictive urge to remain and spoil Raybould's obvious plans, hut he put it down; if this man wanted to make a fool of himself, why not? Besides, he had not yet got over the exhaustion of the previous day, and bed was an inviting thought. He nodded to Raybould:

'I will. I'll have an hour in bed.'

The man's gratitude was almost pathetic. Jerry lingered for a minute or two to watch the snow blasting across the shale face of the mountain behind the caff; it was bad weather for sailors. It was a not unpleasant thought. And when he got to the stillwarm bed, the sound of the wind shaking the roof and the snow driving against the rattling window of the bedroom soon induced a light sleep.

It didn't last long, no more than a few minutes, for Mrs. Raybould's penetrating voice shrilled out from the corridor outside the crowded bedroom; Sukie's excited yelps joined in, and Raybould began to whine in answer:

'She were just earning her keep — '

'Oh, you dirty animal!'

Yip-yip-yip! squeaked the bitch anxiously: *yip-yip!*

Jerry hunched himself into the bed, angry with the Raybolds and feeling the inside of his mouth heavy with a catarrhal deposit. And he had no toothbrush with him!

The Raybolds penetrated the blanket with their quarrel:

'I was just showing her where to get the — '

'I know what you where showing her! You must be mad, at your age! You're dirty, Sam Raybould! If it weren't snowing so bad, I'd throw you both out — like dogs, that's what men are!'

Brenda's voice split the woman's tirade, ice-cold, almost menacing.

'I don't want him,' she sneered. 'He said he were showing me where coal was. Work for my keep like, cos I haven't no

70

money. A bit of that for a bit of breakfast, that's what he wanted.'

'Oh, you dirty, dirty man!' Mrs. Raybould yelled. 'I've worked and slaved to keep a roof over your head and what thanks do I get? I'll not stay in this place, miles from anywhere and your carryings on!'

'I weren't doing anything!'

'You leave that dirty little slut alone, or I'll take the axe to you, Sam Raybould! I've told you before, but you don't listen. Twenty-odd years and you're still the same with those dirty eyes of yours. I'll do for you, I will! Come out! Out!'

'I weren't doing anything!'

The noise heightened to a climax, with the dog yipping and yelping in a delirium of happy excitement. Jerry crawled out of bed, mouth furred and head aching slightly. Days of this!

Finally, the Rayboulds parted, Sam detailed to clean the coffee machine once more and with orders to keep his hands off the slut or he'd find them and worse cut off; the girl snarled viciously in her uneducated voice that she'd had enough.

And there was relative quiet. Even the dog had been silenced. Mrs. Raybould thought so too:

'Sukie, Sukie, Mummy's darling little girl, where is she! Come for her dinner!'

The voice had changed completely' it was all honey and dripping cream, the tones of a thousand telly commercials, indulgent and warm. Sukie didn't answer. Jerry thought he might as well take advantage of the Castle Caffs facilities; he needed a drink to take the night's accumulation of bile away; perhaps Raybould's coffee would do the trick. It was too much to hope that he would have a beer. Or was it?

He went into the uncomfortable dining room. It was very hot, with a glowing red fire heaped up into the black recesses of the wide grate. Brenda was attending it like some priestess, her hand still on the coalscuttle. She turned to Jerry at his limping step but as usual ignored him. Her thin hand trailed over the enigmatic dancing figures in a lover's caress. Raybould looked up, not without friendliness. He looked sheepish and curiously triumphant.

'You wouldn't have a beer, would you?' asked Jerry. 'Or something else?'

'If I had, I'd let you have it. Seeing as it's not regular business. But she won't have it in the place. Nothing like that. I have to go down to Hagthorpe to get a drink.'

'I'll have a coffee then. Isn't Bill Ainsley back?'

Raybould looked out of the window by the door.

'He'll be doing something with the rig. They're all like that. Fussy.' He extracted a brownish stew from the machine. 'One coffee. Brenda!' he called to the girl. 'You want one?'

'Yeh.'

Raybould served her gladly.

Jerry was bored, annoyed, in some pain from his ankle and worried about Debbie. He was also interested in the demoniacal Brindleys; the itch to know possessed him again. Perhaps Raybould's little romantic encounter would make him confidential.

'I was wondering about this Brindley

legend,' he said. 'So they disappeared? When would that be?'

Raybould grinned as he watched Brenda slurping the coffee.

'In the seventeen hundreds and something. Down 'Ag 'Ole.'

'Sukie!' distantly called Mrs. Raybould. 'Oh, where-is-she-Sukie!'

Brenda sneered into the coffee-stew. It was vile, but it counteracted the taste of Jerry's furred mouth.

'Is that all?' asked Jerry. 'I mean, what else?'

Raybould was in the grip of sexual excitement once more. The girl seemed to be able to make him shake like plutonium in an old steam boiler. Jerry gave it up. It would all turn out to be something explicable like the Black Pig of Gautry Pike — Jerry had heard one version of this particular story that referred to a Black Hog, which could have been a corruption of *Hag*, again making it a case of some poor old woman, who, aged and dirty, tried to eke out a living by making up medicines to relieve the pains of childbirth, and, occasionally, stronger brews to get rid of decrepit husbands. So a story some five hundred years old, about a more or less harmless woman, gained supernatural overtones through simple errors of transmission. You couldn't be scientific about things like that. The hell with it! He was considering reading the Western with the missing first chapter when Bill Ainsley staggered through the door bringing a blast of Arctic weather into the overheated room. He was entirely white, frosted over except for his big red face.

'Aye, Sam! Get your missus! Come on!'

He crossed to the fire and unceremoniously pushed thin Brenda out of the way.

'Christ, it's cold! Sam, get your coat on! There's a whole busload of girls out there! Been all night in the bus, and half-frozen!' He looked at Jerry. 'How about you? Can you walk?'

'How far?' asked Jerry.

'Just past my rig — few hundred yards. Half a mile. We'll have to dig them out — they're all moaning and howling and they can't get out to help themselves! Frightened near to death! Come on, Sam!'

Mrs. Raybould came in to hear the cause of the noise.

'Stuck out there?' she said, when she had heard of the trouble. 'A load of girls! What are they doing, out in this weather? There was nothing on the news this morning or last night about them! And why isn't someone trying to get them out from the Hagthorpe side?'

Bill Ainsley slapped his hands together.

'Buggered if I know anything, Missus! They wasn't making much sense, just yelling out for some teacher or something that left them to it! Now, come on! You coming, lad?'

'Right,' said Jerry.

'I said there'd be more!' Raybould complained as he went for his clothes. He returned with gumboots and a huge overcoat. Jerry's anorak was dry, but he was reluctant to face the blizzard so lightly clad.

'Have you got a coat for me?' he asked.

'Don't you go, lad!' said Mrs. Raybould, with a complete change of heart. 'You're badly yourself!'

But Raybould had a spare coat that

fitted tightly, and the three men went to find the emergency gear kept in the cellar. Raybould complained the whole of the time.

'They should pay me — it's this every other week! They said they'd give me a radio if I wanted it, but I wouldn't! Oh, no! Get a bloody radio, and it's Roger this and Roger that and every silly sod that gets lost on the Peak or breaks his bloody funny bone has you then — Girl Guides and damned Pixies. Army cadets and clever bloody coppers tuning in with Z-cars! Not me!'

Jerry recognised the standard boxes of survival gear that had been forced on the unwilling Raybould; he noticed too the vaulted cellars, great arched stonework constructions much bigger than the caff above. There was a musty smell about the place, where there shouldn't be. Limestone was a cleanish-rock. Here was a dirty, age-old deposit on the ground; water trickled down one wall. He could see it clearly in the light of the big torches they found in one of the boxes.

'We want a shovel each,' he said. 'And

we'll take two stretchers. Maybe there's some that can't walk. Flares too.'

Raybould said sourly:

'They'll not see flares in this weather, Oh, no! We 'ad flares when the Boy Scouts went missing, and no one saw 'em in the fog and snow.'

'Sukie-Sukie-Sukie!' called Mrs. Raybould. 'Is she in the cellar?'

'No she bloody isn't!' bawled back Raybould with a grim satisfaction. 'I'd put that bitch on the 'am slicer if I had my way,' he told Bill Ainsley. 'She'd make a good 'am slice.'

'That it?' asked Ainsley, when he had selected the equipment.

'I think so,' said Jerry. 'I'll try to keep up.' They walked to the wide, curving steps that led up to the caff.

'Look at that!' Raybould said suddenly. 'Look at bloody wall!'

Both men stopped, Bill Ainsley with some impatience. Raybould's light played on one of the walls of the cellar. It bulged inwards like a pregnant monolith. There was a hole in the middle of it too, not big, but new, showing where the mortar had been packed about the blocks of stone over two centuries before.

'Must have been a landslip,' said Bill Ainsley. 'I'll swear some of the road down below my rig's gone! Now, come on! Those poor lasses are in a right state!'

Raybould took a step towards the bulging stonework.

'It weren't like that earlier on.'

'Are you coming?' Bill growled.

'Aye! All right!'

Brenda was quite firm about her decision:

'Catch me going out in this lot!' she said. 'Help a set of schoolkids! They can do their own digging!'

'I'll get the blankets ready!' Mrs. Raybould called.

Brenda was resisting Mrs. Raybould's efforts to get her to help when the three men pushed into the howling blizzard. The last Jerry heard was a vituperative shouting from both women.

5

It was the longest half-mile Jerry had ever known. He used a shovel as a prop to relieve the pressure on his ankle; walking in the other two men's tracks was easier than treading into the deep drifts, but it needed all his strength and resolution not to turn back away from the bitter cold and the unrelenting power of the blizzard. It took three-quarters of an hour to reach Bill's enormous red tanker.

'See!' yelled Bill. 'Road's part gone!'

It had. The tanker was set at an odd angle, its nearside wheels a couple of feet below the offside; a whole chunk of road had been carried away into the valley below. They pressed on, this time through still deeper drifts. About a hundred yards further on, Jerry distinguished a small yellow window of the kind used for ventilation; then the neat rounded roof of a Volkswagen minibus.

'I were lucky to see it!' Bill yelled. 'I

wouldn't but they've stuck those out of the window.'

A pair of green tights streamed into the wind, snagged on to the small window in the roof as a signal. When they neared the minibus, Jerry had to lean against his shovel, crippled with pain. The van's roof was partly covered by the drifting snow; soon it would be completely hidden from view. Jerry thought of the terrified girls who had survived one night of freezing terror in that thin metal container; he knew something of their feelings. The chill of the grave possessed him as a memory of hanging by his frozen fingers on Toller Edge came back. He joined Raybould and Bill Ainsley, who were methodically cutting away the packed snow around the lee side of the bus.

Raybould was stronger than he looked. In the overlarge coat, his head and neck swathed in a balaclava helmet and bright orange scarf, he was an energetic scarecrow. Bill Ainsley directed operations. Jerry flung the snow the other two cut out over the top of the drift. Finally, they reached the sliding door of the bus.

The lorry-driver gave a reassuring clang with his shovel on the metal, and for the first time the other two men heard the shouts of the trapped girls. The wind added its own shrieks as it blasted down from the steep sides of Devil's Peak, counterpointing their terrors.

'Don't worry, lasses!' bawled Raybould. 'We'll have you out soon. Jerry! You get those blankets passed along!'

The screams were more insistent now that help was at hand. Someone pushed a hand through the yellow plastic window in the roof, and through the snowed-up windows faces could be seen.

'Told you there'd be more silly buggers stuck up here!' Raybould yelled to Jerry. 'She'll 'ave to 'ave help sorting this lot out! And what's their teacher thinking of!'

Ainsley heaved the last of the snow aside and hammered with the handle of his shovel at the frozen door catches; they gave and the girls set up a howling of relief that momentarily drowned the wind's weird singing. Jerry saw half-a-dozen schoolgirls' faces, all alike — young, sallow, framed with the regulation long, straight hair; all wore bright-looking anoraks with gay sweaters. They had not suffered greatly.

They were full of questions; he caught the words 'Miss Walker-Harbottle' in scared middle-class tones from some of them, but Bill soon shut them up.

'You'll have to walk!' he roared. 'There's a caff not far. Anyone hurt? Anyone frozen?'

There wasn't, they'd huddled together in sleeping-bags, so the girls took the blankets and allowed Raybould to arrange the order of their leaving the van; Jerry caught a whiff of fuggy, stale, air.

More girls emerged, each with her efficient rucksack on its metal grill, each gaily accoutred against the mild English spring. A dozen or so of them made up the straggling party sheltering in the lee of the van. One had a large teddybear clutched in her sheepskin gauntlets; a pretty girl, more so than the others, she tried to ask Bill Ainsley about the Miss Walker-Harbottle they seemed to have lost.

'You what, love?' Bill roared.

'It's our teacher,' three of them screamed with the pretty girl. 'Miss Walker-Harbottle! Have you seen her?'

'No!' Bill roared. 'Where is she?'

'She went last night!' all the girls shrilled. 'When we got stuck! She went for help!'

'Which way?' Raybould wanted to know.

They pointed to the invisible village of Hagthorpe. Bill Aisley looked away. Raybould's face registered shocked justification.

'No use going!' Bill shouted to Jerry. 'Not if she's been gone since last night!'

Jerry knew it for the truth. Either the woman had reached the village, or she was dead. Certainly, they could not struggle on any further through the drifts; their immediate concern must be the girls. Teenagers had no sense: they had to be taken back to safety before they made wrong, irrevocable decisions, like their missing schoolmistress.

'Come on,' ordered Bill Ainsley. 'Leave those,' he told Raybould, who was trying to heft the stretchers across his narrow shoulders. 'We won't need 'em now. You all right, lad?'

Jerry winced. It would be a long walk back up the winding Pennines road. He nodded, fearful of the frozen snow that wanted to tear into his mouth and perform vicious tricks with his teeth.

'Right, girls!'

They emerged, dark figures, from the lee of the van and set off into the teeth of the blizzard that had no right to afflict England now that April was there. Jerry stumbled on at the rear of the column, occasionally gasping with pain. The pretty girl with the teddy looked back once, and when she saw that he was limping, she helped him. Even through Raybould's old overcoat, he could feel the warmth of her plump young body. Brenda had not been able to spare any of her small heat.

'It's terribly good of you to come for us!' the girl shrilled.

'Think nothing of it,' howled back Jerry.

They ploughed in Bill Ainsley's tracks with increasing difficulty. But eventually the grey-black mass of the caff emerged, its walls neatly patterned with sculpted snowdrifts, its too-new roof glittering with frozen snow.

Mrs. Raybould had stirred Brenda into activity of a kind, for the coffee urn belched steam, the fire was a billowing centre of yellow and red heat, and there was the smell of fried bacon seeping into the big, unattractive room. 'Come in! Come in! Oh, you're all frozen! Sam, get them a cup of coffee each! Bill take your things off — girls! Come by the fire!'

The girls stood about for a few moments in an attitude of painful embarrassment. It was Brenda who understood their need.

'The lav's through there,' she said loudly.

As one, they rushed into the corridor leading to the washroom. Jerry could hear relieved yelps and cheerful competition echoing through the building.

'Who are they? Where're they from? Isn't anyone with them?' Mrs. Raybould began. She thought of something else. 'Sam, where's our Sukie? I haven't seen Sukie-darling since you went! She didn't get out, did she? She'd fall into a drift, she would! Hadn't they anyone to look after them?'

Bill steamed luxuriously before the fire.

'Let's have that coffee, love,' he said. 'And pour theirs.'

'Well, get on, Sam,' his wife called.

Raybould struggled out of his clothes.

'Their teacher went down to Hagthorpe last night, that's all I know,' Bill reported. 'We were lucky to find them — they couldn't have got out. The locks on the windows and door were frozen. Mind, they might have been all right for another day or two, as long as they didn't panic.'

Jerry knew that panic.

'Why were they out at that time of night,' he said.

'You never know what you'll get this time of the year in the hills,' said Raybould softly. 'Look at those Boy Scouts. They was out on a hike. And when I first came out here there was a whole busload of old-age pensioners stuck for two days just the other side of the Peak.' He poured thick brown coffee-stew out. 'Two heart-failures and a pleurisy. Who are these?'

'Langdene Academy,' said Bill. 'Down south; Near Worcester.'

'I wonder if their teacher made it?' said Jerry.

Then the girls came back, full of questions, hungry and delighted to be safe. Their sallow faces had been reddened by the snow and wind, and they had combed their hair into long glossiness; they revealed neat, slim figures when they stepped out of the gaily-patterned anoraks. There was a Julie, two Amandas, a Jen, a Peg, a Marie and more equally unmemorable names; the girl with the teddy was Julie. It was she who was concerned most about the missing teacher:

'She said she would bring help! I mean, it was frightfully brave of her — not knowing the road too!'

'No, she didn't,' came a chorus, and the shape of the potential disaster came out.

'Where were you making for?' asked Jerry.

'Why, Landgene Academy's weekend

Cottage at Styal,' they said. 'It's such a sweet little place! You have to get your water from a pump and there's calor stoves and paraffin lamps! We use it as a centre for climbing and walking, but we wanted to do some pot-holing this time — '

'No telephone?' interrupted Bill Ainsley.

'Oh, no!'

'So your school and your parents wouldn't know you were missing,' filled in Jerry. 'What did Miss Walker-Harbottle have on? How was she dressed?'

'Oh, the same as us! The anoraks come from the Camping Club.'

Mrs. Raybould took one of the gay red and yellow anoraks. 'Thin,' she said. 'They look all right, but they wouldn't keep the cold out.'

The girls voiced their fears.

'She'll be all right, won't she?' asked blonde Julie. 'Couldn't we ring for help — information? There is a phone here, isn't there?'

'The lines are down,' Raybould said. 'The electric's next.' He was gloomily delighted.

'But what about our teacher?' Julie said. 'I mean, she'll be all right, won't she?'

The others whimpered, clutching their hot coffee cups for comfort; their eyes widened and they looked at one another with a fascinated horror.

Brenda cracked the silence.

'In this!' she said. 'She's no chance!'

The girls stared at her, noticing the cheap skirt, the grimy thin hands and their tattoos. Brenda sneered at them again and resumed her place by the fire. They left a space around her, but they could not take their eyes off her. She looked down and traced the dancing figures once more.

'Slut!' began Mrs Raybould, but she stopped in the middle of a tirade. 'Listen!'

They all listened. Jerry heard the howling of the wind and the battering of the snow against the top part of the windows.

'What — someone out there?' asked Bill Ainsley.

'Is it Miss Walker-Harbottle?' the girls demanded. 'It is! Listen!'

Jerry could hear something now, a thin wailing as if from a great distance. He went to the door.

'No!' called Mrs. Raybould. 'It's Sukie-darling! Where is she, Sam Raybould!'

Jerry opened the door. Had the dog been let out when they had gone for the trapped girls?

'She's in the cellar,' Raybould said, making for the corridor behind the big room. 'The silly bitch!'

The girls clustered closer around the fire, talking now of the missing teacher; Jerry could see their tremendous preoccupation with the lorry-girl. They tried to include her in their conversations, but she wouldn't allow it. She was aloof from them.

Mrs. Raybould followed Sam. Jerry could hear the sad howling of the bitch clearly, an eerie noise in the darkness of the caff. Then there was a drawing of bolts and Sukie shot in pursued by Mrs. Raybould who was complaining bitterly to her husband at the same time:

'Why didn't you see she was in the

91

cellar! She's delicate, is Sukie-darling! She'll catch her death! Sukie! What's that you've found! Sam!' she screamed. 'She's got a rat!'

'She weren't in the cellar!' Raybould bawled back.

Jerry began to laugh as the bitch chased about the room with something dank and mildewed in its mouth; it must have found the corpse of a mouse or a rat. Certainly it didn't look to have the strength to have overcome even a small rodent.

'Put it down!' ordered Mrs. Raybould.

Bill Ainsley joined in the chase.

The girls called out 'Poor thing!' and 'What's it got?' all thought of their teacher forgotten as the dirt-streaked toy poodle bitch worried at its prize and snarled at its pursuers.

Bill Ainsley caught it by the collar and lifted it to Mrs Raybould. The soggy, torn thing fell. Sukie bit Bill Ainsley's free hand with sharp, frail teeth.

'Sukie, behave, darling!' screamed Mrs. Raybould before Bill Ainsley could cuff it. 'Mind her, Bill, she's a pedigree!'

Bill began to curse, saw the girls watching tensely and stopped himself as a trickle of blood ran down his wrist; Sukie set up a fearful howling, excited and terrified at what it had done but anxious to retrieve her prize.

Sam Raybould stirred it with his foot.

'What is it?' asked Jerry.

'It isn't a rat. Looks like a bit of old wool or cloth.' He bent down and poked at it. Jerry saw green mildew and rotting cloth. 'Hat or something.'

'You mustn't play with nasty things!' chided Mrs. Raybould. 'And why did you leave Sukie down there, Sam! Oh, you swine!' She was angry again. 'She's not to go there.'

'She wasn't there when we left!' he roared at her.

'No, she wasn't,' Bill said.

Jerry agreed, 'We'd have seen her.'

Bill Ainsley offered the bitch to its mistress, who took the yapping, excited creature and allowed it to lick her face. The woman's smile was extraordinary, a young girl's.

'She doesn't like you!' Mrs. Raybould

snarled at her husband, still smiling sweetly at the bitch's attentions. 'You let her in the cellar.'

'I didn't!'

'Then why has she just come from there?'

There was, of course, no answer.

Bill Ainsley poked at the mildewed hat. 'It's a beret,' he said. 'Army. I were Army. We had them just after the war. See there's the badge.'

He disentangled a verdigris-obscured cap-badge from the rotten fabric.

'Where did she find it?' Raybould said. He looked at the dog, which was still excitedly yelping.

'Signals,' said Bill Ainsley. 'See. That's Mercury, the messenger of the gods.' He rubbed the detritus from the metal. 'With his little wings on his feet.'

Jerry felt a cold sensation in the hollow of his back, as if the frozen snow had kept him on Toller Edge; he turned and saw Brenda staring with her mysterious firedark eyes at Bill Ainsley. Jerry said:

'That Army Lieutenant What regiment was he?'

Raybould's face was worried.

'He were Signals. They was a radio unit, testing new radios. We 'ad a storm like this. The others were all right.'

Brenda smiled at the words, and Jerry's sense of unease redoubled. Bill Ainsley looked hard at the girl, but said nothing.

'How could the bitch have got it?' asked Jerry.

They all regarded the hat. Then Raybould turned it over gingerly. The men saw the soiled hank of blonde hair stuck to the leather band.

'It were him,' said Raybould. 'The army said he were big and yellow-haired.' Mrs. Raybould began to understand what the fluffy poodle bitch had discovered.

6

No one wanted to talk about it, but Jerry knew they were thinking the same thing. The white bitch had been in the cellar: where else?

Mrs. Raybould settled the matter for the moment by shouting at her husband: 'She's just found it outside and dragged it in.' No mention of when or how. 'She does that. All dogs do. Sam! Get these girls their bacon butties! Come on! Any of you going to give a hand if you're warmed through'?

'Right, right,' said Raybould. 'Coming!'

The girls noticed the way that the dog's find had been deliberately glossed over; they were curious, but their middle-class politeness won. Julie, she with the long blonde hair and the plump charm, said to Mrs. Raybould:

'Is there any way we can help? We're all trained in House craft. We do Domestic Science.'

Brenda permitted herself a lop-sided smile and Jerry saw the contempt of these girls in her dark eyes.

'Isn't it exciting!' the girls said. 'Of course we'll help!'

They watched Brenda to see what the girl in their new snowbound world would say, they were already fearful of her scorn, aware of her foxy sensuality, her smell of the wild. Mrs. Raybould gave them orders, organising a place for their wet anoraks, seating for them near the roaring fire; they responded like well-brought-up young ladies who could ignore a near-disaster with the best of them. Jerry knew they would sidle back to the enigmatic Brenda when they could.

He was worried. Bill Ainsley recognised it and nodded to him to talk separately from the busy girls as they unpacked their rucksacks and arranged damp sleeping bags over chairs.

'She were through the wall,' Bill said. There was no doubt about it for him. 'That hole in the cellar.'

The mildewed rag still lay on the floor, with the bitch yipping at it from time to time from Mrs. Raybould's cradled arms.

Jerry was besieged by doubts.

'Raybould said the hole was new.'

'Aye! There's been landslips about here for years — it's a fault!' Bill concentrated and mouthed the unfamiliar consonants before trying to say them: 'A geological fault.'

'Could be.'

So where had the bedraggled little bitch been? Through the hole in the cellar and into what part of the labyrinthine caverns that riddle the Peak? He thought of the massive underground rivers that had once blasted their way through the solid rock, carving huge tunnels, eating and grinding away until they emerged in some gentle valley as clear rushing streams full of perch and bream but somehow mysterious to the Peak dwellers who invented tales of monsters — Black Pigs, Green Giants, Grendel Hags — to account for the monstrous holes in the ground.

'They don't want to know,' said Bill Ainsley. He indicated Sam Raybould, who was eyeing one of the girls.

'I don't think I do,' said Jerry,

'Aye,' agreed Bill.

Legends were one thing; you could laugh at the naivety of the Peak dwellers. But a piece of blonde hair and the crusted bit of decaying scalp to go with it was something else.

'We'll report it when we get out,' said Jerry. 'That's all we can do.'

Brenda's harsh voice rang out in the caff:

'Course I do!' she was saying to the schoolgirls. 'They've plenty of money! They're all on the fiddle! They can pay for it!'

Jerry saw the glee of the three or four girls around her. What had they been discussing? They were like rabbits to a ferret. Bill nodded in her direction.

'She knows more than she'll let on. But it's best left for them as can handle it. When's this bloody storm going to blow itself out?'

Jerry wanted to move the mildewed hat, but he had taken a horror of it; he could see the young Lieutenant of Signals stumbling about the Peak in a snowstorm just like this one, and he asked directions and received answers that were wrong for him: and now he was lying somewhere close. And the Rayboulds didn't want to know about it. A primitive terror possessed him, one he could see reflected in Bill Ainsley's eyes and in the refusal of the Rayboulds to recognise what they had seen.

One of the girls had a powerful transistor radio. It belted out music for a while and then the cultivated, concerned newscaster from a wet and cold Manchester rapped out his information:

'The unusually severe weather conditions have taken most parts of Britain by surprise! In the Lake District, the North Riding and parts of the Peak District, high winds and severe falls of snow have resulted in drifts of up to ten feet, making many roads impassable. Motoring organisations and the police have put out warnings to motorists — they should avoid travelling over high ground and watch out for patches of black ice. The gales and exceptional cold will continue for a period of a further forty-eight hours, according to Air Ministry forecasters.'

Brenda was giggling with the girls around the fire. She pointed to Jerry and said something about beards, and he felt uncomfortable.

'Two more days!' Bill Ainsley said. 'Jesus! The rig'll be frozen up! If it's not slipped off the road altogether.'

Jerry avoided conversation. Neither he nor Bill Ainsley wished to make the decision to investigate the cellars under Castle Café. And Raybould wouldn't. Mrs. Raybould had the bitch on a thin chain, Jerry saw. Sukie wouldn't go adventuring any more.

Pop music blasted out from the transistor. The girls were forgetting their terrors. One of them took over the coffee machine, until Raybould complained:

'And who's going to pay, I want to know!'

'Oh, we can pay!' the girls chorused, and they could. They had lots of money. Money was nothing to them. They had Raybould growling with discomfort as they tossed five-pound notes at him. They became more demanding, more assertive.

They wanted chips and eggs, a CD player, if he had one — he was delighted to be able to refuse — and cards, papers, anything to entertain them.

Julie decided that Jerry was worth talking to, so she found out all about him. She told him of their intentions:

'I only came on this crummy expedition because Miss Walker-Harbottle asked me, Jerry.' She knew his name by now. She'd heard of the climb, of Jerry's ambitions to gain a doctorate for finding lost villages, and she had offered him considerable advice as to how to find one or, two.

'You'll have egg and chips, won't you Jerry?' she asked. He refused. 'And you, Bill?' Bill refused. 'Mr. Raybould, haven't you any tomato sauce?'

'No!'

'Oh, well. I was telling you, Jerry. Miss Walker-Harbottle — we call her 'Butch' 'Bottle, she is a bit like that — well, she knew Daddy had done a little geological study some years ago in the Chilterns, so she roped me in as a sort of specialist. Of course I've not done much potholing. I'm more for horses. But none of the others had done any at all, so I suppose I was the visiting expert, sort of. Well!' She hoiked her teddy on to her knee and spread H.P. sauce over her yellowed chips. 'There's a cavern not far from here which we were supposed to look at — oh, Lord, we've got all sorts of duplicated maps and charts to fill in! We're a Field Trip, not just a weekending party. Well! There's this cavern where there's heavy deposits of fluorspar that sort of gives a greenish glow — all eerie, if you know what I mean. It's probably radioactive as all get out. Shall I strap your ankle up?'

She knew first-aid too. Several of them did; there was some competition to display their ability. Four brand-new elastic bandages were produced from the well-stocked rucksacks. Jerry was strapped up, with no cessation in Julie's flow of information:

'Well, it's probably nothing more than an atmospheric effect in peculiar weather conditions, but we were supposed to chart it all. You wouldn't believe it, Jerry, but we're all going to be Young Scientists of the Year if that frightful Walker-Harbottle woman isn't found frozen stiff in a few days' time!'

Jerry shuddered. The cruelty of the adolescent. It was a bore that their teacher might survive. He let her talk on. And he and Bill Ainsley and Sukie glanced from time to time at the gruesome beret. He caught Brenda's interjection, however:

''Ag 'Ole,' she said.

'What!' the girls said, delighted at her pit-village snarl and her dirty fingernails.

''Ag 'Ole,' she repeated loudly, looking for Bill Ainsley's attention. 'It goes green at night sometimes, doesn't it? All greeny after dark.' She smiled and looked down at the coalscuttle. 'Greeny.'

'Yes!' said Julie. 'That's the local dialect expression! Hag Hole! Well! I expect you've seen it too, Jerry?'

'No,' he said, his ankle now well-supported. He got up and left Julie to her plate of pale, worm-like chips. 'Bill,' he said to the lorry-man. 'We've got to see.'

Bill looked at the beret.

'Aye.'

Julie and her friends watched. 'What is it, Bill?' asked a dark-haired girl.

'Something dog dragged in,' said Brenda.

The girls thought this excruciatingly funny.

'It's nothing,' said Bill Ainsley. He took the newspaper and wrapped the rotting beret. 'We'll have a look,' he told Jerry.

'All right.'

'What for?' asked the dark-haired girl. 'I mean, is it something exciting? Oh, do let's come! Brenda was telling us all about it — about the poodle going into the cellar and finding a way through to the caverns.'

'You told them that, Brenda?' said Bill.

She shrugged. 'Why shouldn't I?'

'Well, actually,' said Julie, 'it was me that thought of the connection. I mean, it does seem logical, doesn't it?'

Raybould came in to see Bill holding the grim package. The paper was sodden.

'Can we look in your cellars? Oh, please! We promise we won't touch anything.'

The girls clustered around him, so that

Raybould grinned with a delirious fool's grin. So many young bodies about him!

'No!' his wife yelled, keeping Sukie tight to her bosom. 'Oh, no! I'm not having you lot messing up the place! You should be glad you've got somewhere to shelter — and turn that radio down! I can't hear myself think!'

Something about her reminded the girls of their own acidic schoolmistresses, and they were quiet.

'We'd best look,' said Bill Ainsley to Raybould.

'Do you think?'

Jerry shuddered. 'Yes.'

They went down the narrow, green-painted corridor with its two unshaded bulbs and its sweating walls to the massive barred door. Raybould's wife followed hesitantly. She kept the girls back with a glance, but they peeped from the overheated dining room, giggling and amazed at their own temerity. The bolts clanged back.

'Right,' said Bill Ainsley. 'I'll go down. May as well.' He strove for a reason and found none. 'Coming?'

Jerry followed, with Raybould a reluctant third. The cellar lights were all in good order. Every part of the massive underground store-chamber was brightly lit. They descended the stone steps with some caution, each afraid to admit his fears. Jerry saw that the wall was down.

'Jesus!' Bill Ainsley said sombrely. 'See! Sam, half your wall's gone!'

The bulging wall had fallen. The men could see through a hole as big as two ordinary doorways; the electric light picked out rubble — not the massive stones that had seemed to make up the wall; these were old bricks, once faced with thin stone slabs. The wall at this point was much weaker than the rest of the still-standing building. Through the gap was a tunnel. Its sides, where they could be seen in the steady high-wattage light, were streaming with water.

'See,' said Jerry, interested in the foundations of the wall, for after all this was his trade. 'The water's undermined the brickwork at the bottom. That bit of a landslip must have loosened it, and the cement couldn't hold together.'

107

Bill hesitated. 'What you reckon?' he asked Jerry.

'The bitch must have gone through.'

'Shall we?'

'No!' said Raybould. 'I wouldn't go through there if there was a dozen bloody Pixies lost! Catch me!'

'Well?' asked Bill, ignoring Sam Raybould. 'Jerry?'

Jerry thought of what two years of wet decay could do to the human body. He gulped:

'If there is — if he is — down there, then, well, I feel we should leave it to the proper authorities,' There was a chill slight breeze from the tunnel. Once he thought he saw something pale, like a blob of luminescent fungus, move in the blackness where the light failed.

Bill Ainsley had a slow-moving determination. His big red face was set in an expression of fascinated horror. It was obvious that he would go into the tunnel given any encouragement at all. Jerry could picture the slow, cautious approach: a winding tunnel, then suddenly the entry into the great chamber where rivers had ground the rock away for a million years, and where stalactites and stalagmites formed strange clusters, and somewhere amongst the frozen, dripping rocks, a splayed form, green and long-dead amongst greeny efflorescent frozen rocks! He shook himself.

'No,' he said firmly. 'Not me, Bill.'

'No!' echoed Raybould. 'I'm getting a load of coal up and bolting cellar door. Then some other bugger can go down!' He turned to Jerry. 'It isn't my job! Let them as is paid for it do it! I'll get coalscuttle.'

He ran upstairs.

'What are you doing?' called Mrs. Raybould from the top of the stairs.

Bill Ainsley took a few steps forward until he was amongst the rubble. 'Can't see out,' he declared. 'There's torches in there,' He pointed to the boxes of survival gear.

'What are you doing?' Mrs. Raybould insisted. Sukie added her yapping.

'Nothing!' called back Jerry. 'Nothing, Mrs. Raybould. There's been a bit of a rockfall — a wall down. But we're coming out.'

'There's nothing down there!' the woman shouted. 'Yes, come on, Sam, get them out.' She lowered her voice. 'They've no right down there — now you, hurry yourself.'

'I will, I will, love! I'm filling scuttle and two bags, then I'll come up!'

Bill came up reluctantly. He was annoyed with Raybould and he became sullen. The girls could not draw him out, no matter how much they practised their easy charm on him.

Jerry went for a sleep in the afternoon, tired of the incessant chattering of the girls, tired of the bitch's shrill yappings; he found he soon dropped off into a light doze, and when he awoke it was early evening. Bill Ainsley was snoring in his own bed. The wind still roared over the flimsy roof, and harsh snow attacked the windows. From the dining room, Jerry could distinguish the sound of pop music.

Another one or two days of this!

He washed quietly, careful not to disturb Bill. When he reached the dining room, Mrs. Raybould was making her dispositions for the girls. They would all sleep in the dining room. There were eight mattresses, counting those on the spare beds in the drivers' sleeping-room; the girls could put two mattresses together and sleep three to two of them. They co-operated willingly. Mrs. Raybould ignored Brenda. She could do what she wished.

Jerry saw the girl talking intently to intelligent, plump, blonde Julie. They were completely abstracted. It disturbed him to see that Julie too was allowing her hand to trail on the dancing figures around the elegant coalscuttle. Later, they all played cards, even Bill Ainsley. He taught them a daft child's game called Bing-Bang-Bong, and the evening passed happily enough. Occasionally they stopped to hear the adenoidal Manchester newscaster enthusing about stranded vehicles.

'I wonder whether Butch 'Bottle made it?' one of the girls asked.

'Oh, she's first cousin to the Yeti,' another answered calmly. 'She'll have bedded down in a hole in the snow. They'll find her in a year or so and she'll get up and say, 'Ah, you dear girls! Where have you been?'

They all giggled. Jerry was freshly amazed at the teenagers' malice. Were all women like that at fifteen? Debbie too?

Brenda had increased her group to four now. Blonde Julie was with her still. Bill Ainsley glanced across with a surly expression every so often, for it was easy to guess what the lorry-girl was talking about. Money, men, other girls on the road.

It worried Jerry so much that Brenda should be talking so to the girls that he went to see Mrs. Raybould in her kitchen. She was putting Sukie to bed: there was a tiny hot-water bottle, a pink blanket, and a dish of what looked like liver porridge.

'Are you putting that girl — ah, Brenda — in with the others?' he asked.

'She can do as she likes,' she said in an iron voice to Jerry. 'I told her before. I'll put her out if she gives any more trouble.'

Jerry was stirred to curiosity once more:

'Mrs. Raybould, what Sam was saying about the Brindley legend — '

'I don't know anything about it! He listens to any fool story they tell him

112

down in the pub at Hagthorpe! He's a fool, is Sam Raybould!'

Jerry was lost when talking to assertive women; he knew he was not skilled enough to gain her confidence.

'Couldn't Brenda sleep in the kitchen?' Jerry asked.

Mrs. Raybould ignored him completely, as she fussed with the dog.

Jerry returned to the dining room. Bill was laughing happily, his bad humour forgotten. Brenda was staring into the fire, and so were her new friends. Another night, thought Jerry. Well, he could put up with it. Maybe there'd be a letter from Debbie. Maybe Debbie herself! He would ring from Hagthorpe the next day if the forecasters were wrong; Andy or Anne would look in the flat to see if she had returned from her trip to Shields. If it was a trip.

Mrs. Raybould announced that it was bedtime at half-past ten. The girls at once agreed. Bill Ainsley made for his bed sleepily, and Jerry followed. There had been some discussion as to whether or not they should give up their mattresses

113

for the girls, but Mrs. Raybould wouldn't hear of it. They were her customers, or at least Bill was. The girls were chance strays, with only a problematical payment. At eleven, all the lights in the caff were out.

'What do you make on it?' asked Bill. 'This hole in the cellar.'

'We did the right thing,' Jerry said, lying. 'It's probably nothing at all.'

He lay awake, for an hour, thinking of the girls with their wide innocent eyes and their shocked delight in Brenda's lewd tales. He thought too of Bill's determination to go into the tunnel. For a moment he could visualise the German pilot's face as he lay dying from his burns: cursing the Anglo-Saxons for making a green death-ray in the sky, and knocking the Heinkel out like a broken moth to lie shattered on the shivering mountain. Jerry fell asleep wishing he were a thousand miles from the stone-locked caff, safe with the plump and ebullient Debbie.

He awoke cold, the snow rattling against the window. He hadn't been asleep long.

Bill Ainsley was still and silent. No snoring now, he was deep in sleep. Jerry huddled into the large eiderdown, trying to settle down again when faint noises penetrated his half-sleeping state.

Tiny fluting sounds, full of delicious hysteria reached him. They disturbed him more than anything he could have thought of; there was a blind cruelty about the sounds, as of voles ripping a victim in the dark for the vicious pleasure of it. He sat up. His imagination played tricks: was the noise from the cellar? Was there a something even now approaching with an insidious confidence, a thing that could laugh in this sinister way? A green, long-dead thing?

It came to Jerry with a shock that one of the noises was familiar to him: it was Brenda's contemptuous snarl.

He was immediately angry, and was up on the instant, to shout aloud as he set his weight on his twisted ankle; even so, Bill did not stir.

Jerry's anger increased with the pain. He wrapped the massive yellow eiderdown around him and limped to the door.

There was a light in the dining room. He could see the door part open. He took in the scene in a sweat of fear.

The girls were clustered about Brenda, and it was their half-frightened, half-exultant menacing laughter that had awakened him. And what were they doing!

By the firelight, Jerry could see naked forms in the red firelight, long hair trailing around sharp-boned backs! And Brenda in the midst, crouched animal-like over the brass scuttle, and the figures on it bigger than they should be, the terrible, faceless engravings somehow reflected in the gently writhing bodies of the girls, following the lorry-girl's actions as if she were a dancing-mistress!

Jerry gasped in fright and one girl turned, with fire-dark, red-glistening eyes, but she had not seen or heard him: she was incurious, drugged almost by the heat on her body, drugged into a state of hypnotic trance that centred on the surrealistic dancers on the surface of the ancient brass! Brenda turned too and

Jerry followed the direction of her gaze. He gasped again, controlled his sounds and saw what she was looking at: Raybould!

So Raybould had come along to spy on the girls!

He was crouched behind the coffee-machine itself a gaunt and menacing thing in the flickering light of the fire, and Brenda unquestionably had seen his wet lips and wet eyes, his little scrunched-up features, nose and mouth and eyes all together in a blob in the middle of his white face. Jerry almost crossed himself in an antique gesture of relief, so thankful was he that it was Raybould who had been seen by the strange, menacing skinny lorry-girl. She smiled at Raybould, bared white, sharp teeth at him and deliberately looked away. Then she turned to the fire and whispered mockingly to the girls; and all the girls listened intently.

'They watch and wait,' Brenda said in a tremulous voice.

'We wait!' the others called.

So they were waiting! What for?

Jerry was frozen into utter stillness. He

saw that Raybould was similarly entranced, though more animal emotions caused his stillness. Inside the yellow eiderdown, Jerry shivered with cold.

'Like this!' smile-snarled Brenda, and she moved in a tiny lascivious circle, followed by the whispering girls who smoothly turned towards the brass figures and became one with them.

Their faces too were blank and formless, their lower limbs unshaped, their hair a whirl of darkness. Jerry watched Brenda run her hands down Julie's back, and then the lorry-girl turned and the red mark on her back was an animal thing again, a tiny red rat that clawed at her with sharp movements.

'On the Night?' Julie was whispering. 'The Night? Is it soon?'

Brenda turned to face Raybould, and, without looking directly at him, said harshly:

'They wait unto the Hour!'

And Jerry was aware of an overpowering sense of something coiled and waiting in the dingy room, of something reaching out into the girls' souls and from them to

118

encompass the entire miserable caff and go on to crawl until the whole of Devil's Peak was a shaking, heaving mass of corrupt and horrible malevolence!

Afraid to death, Jerry backed away, not daring to turn for fear of worse. Pressed back by the eerie madness of the girl he knew as Brenda, he stumbled painfully to the drivers' room and found his bed where he lay too terrified to move. Trying desperately to cling to consciousness, sleep took him into grim dreams and imaginings. It was the worst night of his life, the first time since his secure childhood that he had known absolute and unreasoning terror.

He could hear the mournful wailing of Mrs. Raybould's Sukie.

So the poodle bitch sensed the latent power too!

7

Morning brought sunshine streaming through the partly blocked window as Bill Ainsley opened the curtains; Jerry was awake at the slight swishing of nylon, jerking upright with the terrors of the night still on him.

'It's stopped!' Bill said. 'The wind's down, and the sun's out — we'll be out of here today.'

'Thank God for that!' said Jerry.

Bill whistled as he ran water into the washbowl.

'Two or three hours, I reckon, to clear this lot from Hagthorpe, though I can't say how long it's going to be before they get the road mended. Still, you'll be out!'

Jerry was still dazed with relief. No more of the awful dreams that had plagued him since he had slept in the caff. No more of Brenda's haunting powers, no more cellars or caverns, nothing but the companionship of the strays and couples who lived in the huge Victorian tenement near the University where he had been so happy with Debbie. And she might be there, on his return.

'You're quiet this morning,' said Bill,

'I'm still a bit tired. I didn't sleep well.'

'Worried about the cellars?' Bill asked. He turned. 'Funny business, that. Still, it's as well to leave it to the police. If he's down there.'

'Yes!'

Bill looked closer. 'You don't look too good.'

'I'm all right.' Should he tell Bill about how he had been awakened the previous night by an overpowering sense of evil, of how the girls had made waking night-mares ride inside his head? But what could he say? *That they'd been talking and laughing?* Find teenagers that didn't. *Standing around the fire naked?* So they were warming their bits! Debbie did that. Or should he say that Raybould had been there too, and that he too must have seen the figures detaching themselves from the coalscuttle and weaving a monstrous web of *otherness* about the girls? Bill would laugh. Raybould was a notorious Peeping Tom. And patterns in the firelight? How deceptive firelight could be! So what *had* he experienced? A broken dream and a mental state to go with it: the girls were simply robust, normal middle-class girls who talked smut in the dark. And Brenda? He could hear Bill Ainsley dismissing Brenda.

'A cow,' Jerry said aloud,

'Who?' Bill was startled.

'Oh — I was thinking of Brenda.'

'Aye. Best left alone, that one.'

Bill's face, beneath the soap, set in an incommunicative mask. *Had* Bill sensed that strangeness about the girl that so terrified Jerry the night before?

Jerry got up, careful on his swollen ankle — and hadn't the girls been kind enough to dress it efficiently? He felt that he'd been a fool. He'd been a fool on Toller Edge, a fool for not taking notice of Debbie's needs, and a fool for wandering about the caff the night before, at some risk of being accused of voyeurism. He hesitated.

'You didn't wake up last night, did you, Bill?'

Bill shook his head, intent on guiding the razor around the base of his fleshy red nose. 'Why?' he said, the operation complete.

'Nothing. I couldn't sleep. The window's loose. Did you hear Sukie?'

'No.'

Bill mopped his face. 'I'll be glad to be on my way. It's a nasty thought, if he's down there.'

Jerry sweated afresh. He washed his beard vigorously to keep the ice chill away by physical exertion. The fear of the previous night gripped him.

Mrs. Raybould served a poor breakfast. The bacon was finished, so it had to be fried slices of something like dressed tongue. There was rubbery bread and mud-sludge from the coffee-machine. Raybould's head appeared from behind it, as if he had never left its cover all night. The girls thanked him prettily as he passed over the frightful brew; Brenda smile-snarled at him too. This morning it was Julie who sat by the fire stroking the enigmatic figures on the brass scuttle. And over breakfast, Bill Ainsley brought up the subject of the pathetic relic Sukie had found.

'You'll be reporting it to the police, Sam?' he said. The sodden newspaper was on the windowsill beside the two paperbacks. 'That.'

'Reporting?' said Sam. 'It's nothing to do with us! Oh, no!'

'Lot of fuss about nothing,' said Mrs. Raybould. 'I don't want reporters up here. Last time it were bad enough. We even had the telly!'

Sam grinned.

'They couldn't do any filming. 'Ag 'Ole did 'em. It were the radiation, they said.'

The girls began a conversation about their missing schoolmistress, but Brenda listened with interest to Raybould and Bill Ainsley.

'Well, it's best to be sure,' said Bill Ainsley, big shoulders hunched forward with eagerness. 'Wouldn't take more than a few minutes to go down there with the torches.'

The couple refused to answer. Jerry felt

a helpless curiosity afflicting him. Against all reason, knowing himself to be a fool, he said:

'We could take a quick look, Mrs. Raybould. The tunnel looks safe enough. I'd say it's natural rock — the only danger would have been the old wall, but that's down. You wouldn't get a rockfall in a limestone tunnel of this kind.'

Julie looked up and smiled. She had been listening too. 'I'll come,' she offered. 'I've been down a few pot-holes.'

Raybould licked his lips. Jerry could see the ideas forming in his lascivious eyes.

'No!' Sukie began yipping anxiously as her mistress shrieked the word. Mrs. Raybould added:

'I say no, and I mean no! We'll have the wall put back — we'll have concrete, and no more talk of it!'

The girls were silent. Julie began to try to persuade Mrs. Raybould, when a new sound became noticeable, a buzzing and hammering of engines and machinery.

''Elicopter!' spat Raybould. 'They're

'ere again. Soon as the wind drops, *they* come!'

Everyone rushed to the door. On the car park was an amazing sight, a whirling column of snow flung up high into the air by the small helicopter. The noise stopped, and the little machine settled on wide skis. Two large heads poked out, one with a policeman's helmet on it.

Jerry jumped after the others into the deep drifts. The drift was only four feet deep at the front of the caff, protected as it was by the bulk of the Peak behind it; the snow was powdery now, fine and crystal-like in the brilliant sunlight. It was a beautiful morning, with the High Peak a picture-postcard scene: Hagthorpe far below was pure Dickens, and needing only a stagecoach to complete the illusion. Jerry's spirits were raised, the night's oppression gone. He saw that even Brenda had been excited by the sudden visit from the world below. She was in the forefront of the party of girls, all of them trying to talk to the young R.A.F. pilot and the helmeted policeman; neither made any move to leave the machine.

Mrs. Raybould tried to get through, but she was thwarted. It was left to Bill Ainsley to push a way through for her to the plastic bubble and its open windows.

Jerry stumbled along painfully, followed by Sukie, who yipped discontentedly as she sank into the snow. He retrieved her, was bitten, dropped her again and ignored her yelpings after that He was in time to hear Mrs. Rayboold's complaints:

'I've a dozen of them in the caff and one I wouldn't give houseroom to if there wasn't the snow, and there's only tinned pork left and Sukie's not going short for them!'

Sam Raybould had no chance against the girls; the nearness of their young bodies confounded him into silence. They clamoured their news:

'We're the Field Trip from Langdene Academy! Has Miss Walker-Harbottle turned up? You've found her, haven't you! A frozen corpse! Oh, poor brave Butch!'

'Yes, have you seen their teacher?' Bill called.

The police officer, who was known to the Rayb’oulds, called for silence:

'Now, please! One thing at a time, girls! This is the first time I've heard of the lady in question.'

Jerry saw him take a notebook from his pocket. The pilot sat back resignedly whilst Julie gave a full description of the missing schoolmistress, and every single one of the relevant facts. It took fifteen minutes, with Sukie yipping mournfully for attention; Mrs. Raybould went in search of her whilst the middle-class accents rang out crisply in the clear air. The pilot glanced about the plastic blip impatiently.

The sunlight was going. Jerry saw a black cloud beginning to lip over the eerie mask of Devil's Peak, and the pilot hurried the policeman along. He wrote down the details, to the wart on the missing woman's nose. Finally it was done:

'There's more snow coming!' the pilot called. 'Met gives us nine-tenths in an hour or two — I don't want to hang around. We've two more checks yet — ready?' he asked the policeman.

'One moment, sir,' the policeman said.

'Now Mr. Raybould. We know the telephone lines are down. You're well supplied? Let's see, I have the names of all persons at the caff? A Mr. Howard, Mr. Ainsley that we knew about. The twelve young ladies. I have all their names. And — ah — Brenda, that we also know about. You'll not make any attempt to reach the village, now, will you? Most inadvisable! If not dangerous. You should have had that radio, Sam!'

Sam growled discontentedly. Jerry listened as the policeman's official voice droned on. The road was in a very perilous condition. Bill Ainsley's red tanker, far below the caff, was slewed across the road almost completely covered in snow; only the top of the great fat red tank could be seen. It dawned on Jerry and Bill at about the same time that they would return to the caff: that today there would be no return to the world of Deborahs and Snugs.

'I can't leave it much longer!' the pilot said. He was young, impatient, tired. 'We'll be lucky to complete the schedule. Can we go?'

'Anything else we should know, Sam?' the policeman asked. He was near retirement, a dull man who had served Hagthorpe well. 'We'll get your phone back soon, meanwhile I repeat don't any of you try to get down to Hagthorpe.' He looked from Sam Raybould to Jerry, then to Bill Ainsley. 'You'll keep them settled?' he asked the lorry-driver.

'Don't worry,' said Bill.

The machine began to splutter into life, and the girls shrieked at the blast of noise.

'Another thing!' Jerry yelled to the policeman who was pushing his window closed. 'There was this beret — the Army officer! We didn't tell you — '

Steel whirred, the engine whined, and the policeman's red face was grave and serious as he tried to listen through a hundred decibels to what the bearded young man was saying; the habit of attention, product of thirty years of policing, was with him though he had no chance of hearing the words, no chance at all; and Jerry talked on as the machine rose into what was left of the sunlight, up into the cold air and across the face of Devil's Peak so that its shadow crossed the eerie horns like an insect brushing across a beast's face, a passing nuisance. The clouds thickened, and Jerry saw that there would be snow.

8

'I say, Brenda, won't it be fun to stay another night!' rang out Julie's fastidious voice.

The lorry-girl turned and headed for the caff followed by the trail of excited schoolgirls, her dank hair blowing about in the increasing wind. Bill Ainsley and Jerry followed.

'I tried to tell that policeman about the Army fellow,' Jerry said. 'He wouldn't listen. No one listens.' His apprehension increased as he saw Brenda laughing with Sam Raybould at something Sam had said. 'You're sure you didn't hear anything last night?'

'Why?'

The two men readied the caff, to hear Mrs. Raybould yelling at her husband for allowing Sukie out into the snow; Raybould hid from her.

'Listen,' said Jerry urgently. 'I think there's something going on here! I'm sure

132

of it. I expect you noticed how Brenda seems to have got the girls into a weird way of giggling and talking?'

'She was telling them how much she makes on a good night,' said Bill. 'They'll have heard worse.'

'She's doing more than that.'

They were about the fire once more, talking in low tones. Raybould appeared from time to time from the corridor, eyeing Brenda.

'Aye?' Bill wasn't especially interested.

'I got up last night — I couldn't sleep. It must have been around midnight. I heard this noise — it was them! They were in a trance, Bill, a trance! She'd got them into some kind of hallucinatory state — '

'Oh, Lord!' rang out a clear, educated feminine voice. 'How could you, Brenda!'

And the low growl of South Yorkshire went on, to describe some motorised adventure of the Ml.

'How d'you mean?' said Bill. 'Like what?'

'Well, they ware all naked — and that damned coalscuttle was in it! You know how the firelight catches the figures and seems to make them move?'

'It's a bit fanciful — '

'I didn't imagine it!' Jerry said fiercely. 'They were in a trance — and Brenda was showing them how the figures should move. I tell you, Bill, she's evil! The girl's got something about her, that turns these girls the same way! Anyway,' he said, remembering Sukie's mournful howling, 'the poodle sensed it. *She* was awake.'

'The silly bitch howls at nothing,' Bill grinned. The driver looked at the happy, chattering group. And Jerry could see his difficulty. The evidence of his own eyes flatly contradicted what Jerry was saying; some of them started up a game of Bing-Bang-Bong; two were rereading the agony column of *Woman*, and Julie was telling Brenda about school. They were all so normal!

'I didn't dream it!' Jerry insisted.

'They do get a bit like that, all girls together,' Bill allowed. 'Clothes off after dark, like.'

'But the sensation of evil!' Jerry exclaimed. 'And what about her and that missing Lieutenant?'

'Aye, well, there wasn't much to that. He lost his way. She'd been around, so naturally when the call went out one of the drivers who'd picked her up mentioned it, and she was questioned. But she'd nothing to do with it — he must have been trying to find the tracks around the other side of the Peak. There was this radiation that kept mucking up his radio. So he went to look at the Hole. He wouldn't be able to find his way down — the lower tracks aren't too clear and there was a bad mist; no, it was all talk.'

'Sam Raybould saw it!' Jerry burst out, trying to keep his tones low. 'He was there! He saw it all — the girls dancing; the figures in the firelight!'

'Aye, Sam would,' Bill smiled. 'He'd get an eyeful if he could.'

'But what about the coalscuttle! It was part of the fittings of the old Castle! It must mean something together — the dancers, Brenda, the Lieutenant!'

Bill was becoming impatient.

'Don't let it bother you too much, lad. You don't think right when you've been stuck out in this snow for days.' His eyes strayed lustfully to Brenda, who smiled her animal's grin at him and watched him sweat.

Jerry got up in anger. He had been dismissed. Refusing to join in a game of dominoes, he went in search of Sam Raybould as the wind began to shake the roof and the windows; snow slid off the roof where it had piled high. Jerry could see the silent movement of white darkness as it went.

Here was an accumulation of pointers to plain, everyday evil! Jerry would find the clue to it all! Wasn't he trained in research?

'Mr. Raybould!' he said excitedly, when he had run the caff-owner to earth in the little kitchen. 'What were you saying about these Brindleys? Now, precisely *when* did they disappear?'

Raybould sniffed. 'Bugger the Brindleys! What about that policeman — he'll want to know where the stretchers are! Some sod will have them on a lorry as soon as the snow goes, then it's me that'll have to pay!'

'Stretchers?' said Jerry in confusion.

'Aye! Them as Bill Ainsley said leave at the school bus! They'll not be there long! I'm 'aving that Mountain Rescue stuff out — all of it! They can keep it down in 'Agthorpe!'

The petty things that occupied simple minds! Jerry restrained his impatience.

'Don't you think it needs investigation, Mr. Raybould — this cavern the cellar leads to? The tunnel we saw. It should be investigated! It may well be that the legend you heard of in the pub has some basis in fact — there may be underground chambers you know nothing of! And think of the lost treasures of Tutankamen!'

'What?'

Jerry felt he had made contact; Raybould's wet eyes were inquisitive now, not hostile. 'That tunnel wasn't blocked off by accident, you know!'

'The tunnel?'

So Raybould could bring himself to admit there was a tunnel; Jerry pressed home his advantage.

'Think of the satisfaction of being the

first to see what the builders of the Castle wished to conceal!'

Raybould thought about it. Sukie sniffed around his feet trailing her length of chain.

'All right,' he said. 'It wouldn't do no harm. Don't touch anything, mind! I don't want them interfering sods saying I've been at their boxes!'

'So we can look?'

'*You* can.'

Jerry had not conceived of going by himself. There was the horrifying beret to consider. And the terrors of the night. He steeled himself.

'Right. I won't be long.'

So, amazed at his own courage, Jerry limped along the corridor and unfastened the bolts on the cellar door. He turned on the lights. The dank air was cold and unpleasant. The harsh, unshaded lights illuminated every corner of the vast vaulted chamber; he turned to the pile of rubble with its uninviting rough entrance to the tunnel beyond. It was darkly menacing.

'Torch,' he said aloud. He looked back to the cellar door. He had left it part-closed so that there would be no interference from Mrs. Raybould. Or her poodle bitch.

He selected a big electric torch from the Mountain Rescue gear, checked that it worked and limped to the rubble. Something slid along the wet heap of old cement and brick: Jerry saw a snake-like trail of water oozing through the new heap of detritus. He swallowed nervously and flashed the light ahead.

The tunnel was obviously worked. So his first impression had been wrong. The marks of the pick and the blackness of powder still marked its sides and roof. He stooped suddenly, aware again of a blob of luminescence glowing greenly in the white radiance of the big reflecting torch. It was a piece of rock, again a worked piece, one left over from the construction of the thin wall. He walked on.

A slight sharp noise stopped him. All his terror returned. He was at the corner now. One more pace and he would be beyond the range of the electric lights of the cellar: in absolute darkness, totally reliant on the torch.

'A rat,' he said. Then: 'No.' There'd be no rats. Rats needed a food-source. He thought of the missing Lieutenant and backed away, stumbling in his haste.

He stumbled on around the turning before he could recover from his mental turmoil. And there was the thing he knew he did not wish to see.

'No!' Jerry yelled.

But the light would stay on the terrible scene and he was rooted to the spot by an appalled and excruciating horror.

The light flickered strongly in his shaking hand. It showed the end of the wide, high tunnel, a natural river-made tunnel this, which led far away into the distance: and it showed too the small oaken door with its massive iron bars where those who had sought and found Hag Hole had perished!

Green in the radiance of the light was the face of the Army Lieutenant, still with his blond hair to identify him, still with his combat jacket on and his big ungainly boots out of which stuck bone and decaying flesh. Jerry tried to move but he could not make his legs operate. He shivered, shook, groaned slightly and found that horror had him in an unshakeable grip: he closed his eyes against the sight, but still he could see it!

Two small corpses stretched out bony arms to the doorway. There was a clasp knife in one decayed hand. And the others! Who were they? How had they come to find death here in this underground hell! Jerry found himself moving forward, not backward. It was as though there could never be relief from the frightfulness of the pathetic things scattered about the smooth, shining wetness of the tunnel floor.

There was a figure in such old fashioned clothes that Jerry had difficulty in dating them: a cutaway coat, a high hat that was mildewed but still retained its jaunty shape of how long ago? A century? More? It was a smallish, oldish man, for some of the face was still there — and then Jerry saw the Boy Scouts who had tried to use their undeveloped ability to survive in this grim and deadly place! How little Baden-Powell had done for them!

Jerry looked at the door. It was marked with cuts and scratches. *The boys!* Jerry shone his light and saw that the blade of the clasp knife was broken. He looked closer at the door. There was a dark keyhole. What lay beyond?

He shuddered and then jerked back on to his cruelly-aching leg with a new surge of absolute horror: for he had seen indentations in the old iron-hard wood that could only be teeth marks! These lost creatures had tried to bite their way to apparent safety! He looked about wildly. *What had he found?*

The police would have to know! And, God, what would the parents of the boys have to go through — agony afresh if they got to know of this grim end!

Jerry turned, stumbled and fell, losing the torch.

The torch was a couple of yards away. He crawled to it as to a sanctuary.

There was something in his way, something moving with him against his right hand. He pushed it, felt mouldly wet leather and shook his arm free of the clinging stuff, but it wouldn't go and his wrist was entangled in straps and he couldn't quite see what it was, for the light was in his eyes and he had to get out! The thing stayed with him as he groped for the torch, trailing behind him wetly.

He turned the corner of the awful tunnel and ran lopsidedly down towards the cellar, pursued in imagination by the silent green ghosts behind; he gasped as he fell once more, this time over the rubble brought down by the landslip. It wasn't until he was in the cellar that he realised that the lights had been turned off.

He launched into a shambling run for the steps. 'Mr. Raybould! Put the lights on!'

He crawled up the stone steps, the leathery wet straps still wound around his wrist, though he was not aware of the entanglement by this time. Neither did he realise that the clinging and rotten material was parting and that the small satchel he had inadvertently dragged with him in his flight was free of the retaining straps; he was almost oblivious to all except the frenzies of terror. 'Help!' he screamed as he reached the heavy cellar door. 'Let me out!' The big torch fell from his nerveless hand.

He found the handle as the torch bounced into extinction on the stone floor below, shattering and dying in a moment. The nails of his fingers broke, pain dazzling him with another kind of brightness.

9

'It was open all the time,' Mrs. Raybould said. 'Look at your hands! And your clothes!'

Jerry was still an object of some fear in the large room where Bill Ainsley and Raybould had brought him. Mrs. Raybould kept Sukie from licking his face, but the poodle bitch yipped as Jerry struggled to find words to describe his experiences.

'Where've you been?' she demanded of Jerry. 'You'll have to wash your clothes! And what's that smelly thing you've got?'

'Yes!' agreed the girls, coming closer, their nice faces aglow with pity. 'Poor Jerry, what's the matter?'

He cowered from their amiable smiles. Brenda saw his fear — he knew she saw it, for she smiled her smile-snarl at him, especially for him.

'The door!' he got out. 'Bill, the door!'

'It weren't locked!' Raybould said. 'I

wouldn't have locked you in! What's matter with you!'

'The lights! You turned them out!'

'No!' answered Raybould. 'It's the electric — snow's got the lines down in Hagthorpe. Always does when there's this.'

Raybould disliked this show of helplessness. An inadequate man himself, he loathed any reminder of another's need. Jerry saw annoyance in Mrs. Raybould's face, and something near contempt in the lorry-driver's. The girls showed awe, an unpleasant satisfaction somehow; whilst Brenda stared with her smoke-dark eyes like some seer quite happy so far with her arrangements.

Jerry found lucidity in the depths of his despair:

'There's a whole heap of dead people down there!' he yelled. 'Not just one.' He stared around the faces and looked down at his torn fingernails. 'There are! *He's* there — he's green, but he's there, and the hair's the same, my God, the hair's there and it's blond! And his big bloody boots! *And* the Boy Scouts, they *are*!'

'Hush!' Mrs. Raybould commanded, but she was talking to Sukie. 'Hush-and-don't-smell-at-the-nasty-mouldy-things!'

Bill Ainsley looked for support to the schoolgirls. Julie was prompt with advice.

'A trauma!' she diagnosed. 'It is, isn't it, girls? Dr. Muller said it was when they go like this — they can't distinguish between a waking nightmare and a genuine unpleasant occurrence. She's our G.P., you know. She gives us talks. She's qualified as a psychologist. Look at him! All the classic symptoms!'

She moved towards him and got a whiff of the graveyard stench from the slimy leather strap still wrapped around Jerry's wrist.

'Ugh!' she said. 'A trauma!'

'Oh Jesus, can't you listen!' Jerry wept. 'It's true! They were trying to break the door down! They thought that was the way out!'

'Bed,' said Bill unsurely. 'He needs a doctor.'

'Well he isn't going to 'ave one,' said Raybould. To Jerry he bawled: 'You've had a shock but you've got to bloody behave, or I'll belt you one!'

Jerry stiffened.

'No, you won't,' said Bill Ainsley.

'That's something at least,' Jerry got out calmly enough. He relaxed and lay back before the big fire. 'Listen,' he said almost in a normal voice. 'It's all true. There is something down there. I counted four corpses.'

The girls shrieked. This wasn't delirium.

'Oh, no,' said Mrs. Raybould. 'There can't be. We'd have known.'

'Yes,' agreed Raybould. 'We've been 'ere more than twenty year.'

Bill Ainsley relaxed in turn, releasing his grip on Jerry. Brenda was uninterested, Jerry saw. Her eyes were on the engraving, her thin fingers weaving the familiar hypnotic patterns over the dancers.

'He's seen something,' said Bill. 'It'll have to be reported.'

''E'll 'ave to be reported,' Raybould insisted. 'There's nothing wrong with Castle Caff.'

But there was, thought Jerry, and he was beginning to be frightened again. He recalled now the slight dragging weight of the thing that had wound itself to his wrist and shuddered. But, thank God, it was gone!

'He has seen something,' Bill said again.

'Undoubtedly!' Julie agreed brightly. 'I mean, trauma doesn't come from nothing, does it?'

'We could look?' Bill said.

'No!' Mrs. Raybould shouted. 'Sam! No one goes down!'

'There was the beret,' said Julie softly. 'I mean, it is a fact, isn't it?'

'Fact?' Raybould spluttered. 'It's nothing — and you lasses shouldn't be concerning yourselves!'

Brenda called them over. They clustered about her as Jerry was led away to bed by a much-disturbed Mrs. Raybould, Sukie and Bill following.

'Bill!' Jerry called, sitting up once Mrs. Raybould and her dog were gone. 'Just a minute!'

Bill was willing to stay. 'You all right now?'

'I'm all right! I was frightened out of

my wits — look at my nails! Those poor devils down there had been scrabbling at the door like animals!'

'You did see them?'

'Yes! I told you — there was the Army fellow, and the Boy Scouts! Bill, who's going to tell their parents! It isn't so bad about the others — there's one down there that most have been lost for a hundred years! I couldn't recognise the clothes, but they're really old!'

Bill was very interested. 'I thought at first you were, like, a bit round the twist — but I'll have a look now! I will!'

'Not just now, Bill. There's more to it than people being lost!'

Bill wanted to be away.

'Wait, Bill, don't you see, *Brenda's* in it too! I haven't got it all yet, but it's beginning to fit together — even the dates! And the way she's got the girls going!'

Bill's face became almost contemptuous. Where Brenda was concerned, Bill could see only one thing.

'What about the dates when things happen around here! It's always the same

— about this time of year! It isn't just a coincidence, Bill. Schliemann worked it all out through distances. That's how he found Troy!'

'Aye?'

'It was all in the legend — Homer!'

'You'd better get some rest. I'll have a look for myself. And if it makes you feel better, I'll keep Brenda out of it. And the lasses.'

Jerry had lost his interest. How could you convince the uneducated that the source of a legend must necessarily be rooted in fact? That however distorted the elements of the story might be, no one could make the intellectual leap to invent something quite new!

'Hang on, Bill! Listen! When was it the Army Lieutenant went missing? I'll tell you! The end of April! That was when we had fog in Sheffield! And what about the Boy Scouts? They went last year when we had snow like this — in April, right at the end of the month!'

'So?'

'That Nazi bomber — wasn't that at the end of April too?'

'*That* was,' agreed Bill.

'So the dates fit together!'

'Aye, well, what do they fit?'

'I can't remember!' Jerry said in anguish. 'Bill, don't go for a minute — ask Sam Raybould about the Brindleys! Ask him when they went missing!'

'Who're they?'

'Just ask him!' Jerry cried. 'The date! And get me a diary!'

Bill shrugged, and promised to do as he was asked. Jerry thought he had managed to re-engage his interest, but he was not sure; above all, Bill Ainsley wanted to see for himself the sights of the cavern.

Bill returned to find Jerry huddled in the clothes and staring at the snow. The wind rattled against the glass. There was a sense of confinement about the room, almost that of a nineteenth-century asylum for the insane.

'Here's your diary,' he said.

'The Brindleys!'

'Aye, well, he told me about them. What he'd told you — he didn't want to, but we went out of the kitchen and he did. She won't let me go down there.'

Jerry was utterly relieved. The cellar could stay bolted until it was investigated by people in uniforms.

'The Brindleys?' Jerry asked, searching with torn fingernails for the page he wanted.

'He wasn't sure. But it was about this time of year, and in a snow like this. There's an old woman who tells the stories in his pub — '

'Jesus!' Jerry passed the diary, with trembling fingers. 'Look!'

The lorry-driver read the outlandish syllable. 'Wal — Walpurgis — Walpurgisnacht?'

'Walpurgisnacht,' Jerry repeated. 'It was the most powerful of the Old Religion's Sabbats.' The date was marked in red. 'Whose diary is this?'

'Well, it's mine, Jerry! How are you?'

Jerry flinched when he heard the cultivated and concerned tones. Julie smiled down at him.

'I thought I'd look in. I've brought a coffee.'

Jerry shivered. The girl's bright eyes disturbed him unutterably.

He closed his eyes and heard the lorry-driver advise the girl to go away,

When he was sure she had gone, Jerry looked out from underneath the bed-clothes where he had hidden.

'You shouldn't have let her know!' he gasped. 'Not her — she'll be telling Brenda now! Bill, for God's sake take care! Did she hear the rest of it?'

'You're bloody daft, lad! But I don't know, you've had a hard time! Even if there are corpses down there, it shouldn't trouble you. Get some sleep, lad — you best rest while you can! Forecast is it'll start thawing tomorrow!'

Bill Ainsley left without another word, and Jerry snuggled down into the blankets to hide his anger, his solitude, his apprehensions. He heard the blast of pop music as Bill joined the girls in the big dining room. He thought he could hear Raybould arguing with his wife, but the words were muffled. He tried to sleep and achieved only a partial suspension of consciousness.

The trouble was the wind. It moaned and howled off the slopes of Devil's Peak, driving the frozen snow with it to sweep down to the picturesque village below; and wind and snow would scratch and rattle against the window, rat's paws, vole's teeth, bringing unpleasant associations and memories that were best left in their coffins.

Steps sounded in the bedroom, louder than the gusts of wind. Something tugged at the bedclothes. Jerry sat bolt upright, expecting Brenda to appear with the girls.

He opened his eyes and saw Mrs. Raybould's gaunt face. She had red-rimmed, angry eyes.

'What have you been saying to Sam?' she demanded. 'He isn't himself, going on with that Bill about the cellar! And the girls! They're on to me all the time, wanting to go down and see the Castle Cemetery! That's what they're saying! You tell them you were only joking, that you were only having them on. Leave the eiderdown alone, Sukie-darling!'

Jerry felt pity for the woman. She so desperately wanted disbelief when her husband, Bill and all the girls had accepted the truth. He recalled his own earlier scoffing at Sam Raybould's chance-heard stories of the cavern called Hag Hole and felt renewed pity for her. Wouldn't it be better to offer her some comfort, at the expense of a little prevarication?

'Maybe I was a bit off my head at the time,' he lied. I was in a bad way, wasn't I, Mrs. Raybould? You can make yourself fancies up when you're scared, you know. Yes! That's probably it — leave the damned door shut, and we'll forget about it!'

'That's all right, but all those snotty-nosed kids won't! They keep asking that slut to take them on a guided tour! They're horrible, horrible! And Sam's encouraging them — he's told them all about Hag Hole! They say they're on a pot-holing trip; or something and we should let them down, especially because there's something nice and juicy to see!'

Jerry felt a cold hand clutching his heart.

'You keep the cellar door bolted, Mrs. Raybould!'

'Oh, I will! They won't get in,' she

asserted, but she was afraid of their middle-class superiority. She bowed to it, to some extent. 'They'll be wanting chips again. That's all I've got left, beans and chips.'

She went, Sukie's chin in her hand. Jerry dressed, looked outside and saw the last of the daylight greyly disappearing through the glare of the snowfields. He went to the light-switch and remembered there was no power.

In the dining room, illumination was provided by a large oil-lamp and half-a-dozen candles. The girls clearly enjoyed the novelty.

'Jerry, Jerry, how *are* you!' the girls welcomed him. 'What do you think! Miss Walker-Harbottle has been rescued! Really! Old Butch was found with a lorry-driver — she's been there since Friday night! It was on Radio Manchester! She'd set out walking and fallen and been trapped somewhere on the Manchester road, and she'd shacked up with this man. Our Butch! She was on the newsflash just now! She'll never live it down! I mean, our French mistress is potty over her, and she'll be disgusted at the thought of Butch with a big lorry-driver for two nights!'

Bill Ainsley was talking to Brenda. Jerry saw her, and her smile of agreement. The driver was besotted, entirely hers.

'Won't you take us down to see the catacombs?' pleaded dark-haired Amanda. 'Yes, Jerry *dear*?'

'Please, Jerry! I mean, here we are, all ready for a bit of the speleology and nowhere to do it! Do be our guide, darling Jerry!' Julie wailed.

Jerry muttered something in negation.

There was a silence and Jerry saw the reason. Brenda and Bill Ainsley were making for the corridor. The girls were hypnotised by the sight. They had forgotten Jerry. Their lips were wet; their eyes preternaturally bright. Jerry shuddered, looking at Brenda's retreating back. Then he recalled the strange cicatrice at the base of her spine.

He knew that he had to convince the Rayboulds and Bill of their danger. That much he owed them.

10

Jerry ate his plate of baked beans and worm-like chips without relish, though the girls displayed healthy appetites. They splashed sauce liberally until Raybould appeared from behind the sludge machine to complain about their excessive consumption. They giggled openly at him. Julie scrunched her features at him and said:

'We 'aven't 'ad all of it, Mr. Raybould. 'Ave we?'

The others thought this mockery delicious; Raybould joined in their laughter, freshly hypnotised by their young limbs. They could mock him all they wished: he gained something from the exchange. Mrs. Raybould asked if they wanted cakes and coffee, and of course they did. It was only then that she realised that Bill Ainsley and the girl had gone missing.

She looked about the poorly-lit room

like a broody hen:

'Where is she?' she muttered. 'Sam?'

Raybould glanced at the corridor leading to the drivers' bedroom. 'I don't know, do I? I'm not supposed to look at 'er I'm not!'

'He's gone too,' she said. 'Bill Ainsley.'

The girls clamoured for cakes, but Mrs. Raybould was amazed and annoyed. Raybould enjoyed the scene.

It was dark outside — dark too early, the night approaching fast. Already Jerry could sense the girls' excitement. They were feral, night creatures now, they were stacking away bread and margarine, pounds of fried chips, thousands of beans in orange sauce, mud-sludge-coffee, stale éclairs, bars of chocolate: they were preparing, like any night creature, for activity. And Brenda? What was she doing?

'He's at her!' Mrs. Raybould had decided. Sukie perked up, sensing a romp. 'She's at it — here! After all I said!' She picked up a candle set in a lemonade bottle, then stormed away, candle flickering, the girls dizzy with delight. They turned to one another, glanced at Jerry to see what he made of it, turned then to Raybould to watch the envious sickness on his features — and then dissolved into bright laughter.

'She'll catch it,' Raybould said with satisfaction.

That was all very well, thought Jerry, but why was the lorry-girl making herself available *now*? Obvious! She knew that Jerry had seen her! She knew that Jerry suspected her part in the Signals lieutenant business! Jerry looked about the girls helplessly. He saw Raybould's foolish grin as they laughed at the Rayboulds' discomfiture and waited for the explosion from the drivers' bedroom.

'Out!' screamed Mrs. Raybould from the corridor at last. The girls were silent. 'Out, you nasty little bitch!'

Sukie joined in. Raybould found Jerry's eyes and muttered:

'She won't have it in the caff — not at any price!'

Brenda was pursued into the caff by Mrs. Raybould. The girl was calm, her hair disarrayed and hanging lankly about her thin shoulders. She had dressed quickly, with woollen socks not quite in place, face showing twin patches of pink in her sallow cheeks, eyes smouldering with unsatisfied lust, Mrs. Raybould, gaunt and tall, was a fury.

'Get her out, Sam!' she stopped as Brenda wasn't into the midst of the group of girls. They closed around her, not laughing, not smiling, but wide-eyed and quite apologetic. 'Get her out of here!'

'Can't love! It's still snowing! And didn't Arthur Rowbotham say we shouldn't let anyone leave? We'd be responsible! Calm down, Sylv!'

Mrs. Raybould's breath came less furiously.

'That Bill Ainsley will never stay here again! Not after this! And she'd better not set foot in my caff again — never! She's wicked!' She turned to Jerry: 'Would you put up with it?'

'No!' Jerry said, with feeling. He saw the wild hate in the girl's eyes and modified what he had said. 'That is, I can quite see why you're disturbed! It's not conventional behaviour, Mrs. Raybould.'

'Best keep out of 'er way, Brenda,' warned Raybould. 'Don't bother 'er again. Sylvia! Come and have a cup of tea in the kitchen, love.'

'Yes,' agreed Jerry, seeing his chance to try and convince the woman of his suspicions. 'Mrs. Raybould!' he called, following her. 'Can I talk to you for a minute? You and Sam?'

The kitchen was quite inadequate to cope with even a small family's cooking, but it had produced the mountainous heaps of chips for the girls. How? Mrs. Raybould was opening a can of Dog Delight for Sukie, Raybould was trying to make a pot of tea, and Sukie was yipping with anger at the delay. She wanted the tea.

'You're 'ere,' said Raybould. 'I'm not 'aving it! That bloody cellar stays bolted!'

'Yes, yes, I said it should — I told your wife that was the only way to avoid trouble.'

'You've made enough!' Mrs. Raybould told him, joining cause with her husband. 'You and your stories!'

'Mrs. Raybould, that's what I've come

to see you about — the, ah, stories. You see, there *is* something going on — and it is connected with my discoveries!'

As he said it, Jerry realised he might just as well be talking to himself. There was no communication, none!

'Oh. Sukie — here's your tea!'

Jerry clung to straws.

'She knows!' he said, fondling the skinny bitch. 'Sukie knows! She won't go near Brenda because dogs are psychic — '

'There's nothing wrong with Sukie!' Raybould said, sensing more adverse criticism of Castle Café. 'She were wormed last month. And we 'ad the vet!'

'No,' said Jerry. 'I didn't mean she's ill — it's just that she's unnaturally sensitive!'

'She's all right!' Raybould snarled.

'But she's sensitive, Sam,' said Mrs. Raybould, who knew the word. 'She is peculiar about people. Do you mean she doesn't like — *her*?'

'Yes,' said Jerry, knowing he had communicated. 'Sukie darling knows she's a bitch.'

'Well,' said Mrs. Raybould. 'Sukie-darling knows!'

'The other night — last night! Didn't Sukie howl? I heard her! There was a reason, Mrs. Raybould! You must have known she was frightened!'

'She had wind,' Mrs. Raybould explained. 'She suffers from it. That's why she has hot tea.' The woman remembered something else. 'You were up in the night,' she accused her husband. 'Where were you?'

'Ah!' Sam said, terrified. 'Ah!'

'He was making up the fire,' Jerry helped.

'Yes! Coal on the fire!'

Raybould's features contorted themselves in a prayer for silence. Jerry, knowing he was a fool, granted it and said no more about Raybould's peeping. But they had to be brought face to face with the rest of it. They deserved to be told of their peril!

'Mrs. Raybould, can't you see that Sukie knows more than we do? I mean, didn't she come back with the beret?'

'Beret!' said Mrs. Raybould. 'What's

that to do with *her*?'

'I don't know, Mrs. Raybould,' Jerry said. 'But she did send that poor devil down Hag Hole!'

Mrs. Raybould struggled with her hatred of the lorry-girl. She dearly wished to implicate her,

'Well!' she offered, undecided.

'Think of the coincidences, Mrs. Raybould! There was the Army Lieutenant — that was late April. Then the Boy Scouts last year in the snap storm, just about this time. And the Heinkel being pulled down in the war — that was late April! And now, here we are, right at the end of April again!'

The Rayboulds stared at him with such blank incomprehension that Jerry was appalled. How could people be so unintelligent!

'Wait!' he said. 'I'll get the beret! And if that doesn't convince you, you'll have to go into the cellars yourselves — ' He brushed past Bill Ainsley who was standing hesitantly outside the kitchen. 'And there's that Brindley business!' he said over his shoulder.

'Aye, lad — ' Bill Ainsley said, but he was gone.

Jerry opened the dining room door, full of resolution, determined once and for all to end the farce, to bring these uneducated people to the light of reason. He gasped when he saw the girls clustered around the coalscuttle. He blanched when be saw that the candle flames were wavering, that Brenda had the group around her swaying slightly. There was a whiff of corruption in the dingy room, a hint of foul and unburied things.

The beret!

Against his will, he moved forward, but the girls took no notice.

'Excuse me!' he said loudly, pushing past Amanda. Her body was iron-hard against him, but his strength prevailed. She gave way and he was in the middle of the group, and Brenda was before him crouched over the eerie scuttle, and *things* crawled about the unclean floor, writhed, crawled in shadowy patterns between the fire and the great brazen container. The mildewed and pathetic beret was there, unwrapped, before the coalscuttle, as though it were an offering. And Brenda traced little movements above the dancing figures, weaving them into unsure lines and cloudy emanations which filtered through to the deep areas of Jerry's mind, grasping at primitive, forgotten fears and entering with a vice-like grip into the depths of his entire being! There was a growing evil in the circle of faces. Healthy schoolgirl complexions were dark, remote, mysterious, and threatening in the dim oil-light; their thin bodies swayed to Brenda's slow-moving hypnotic tattooed hands, and they moved and bowed to the decaying trophy before the fearful brass scuttle.

Jerry tried to move, but again a firm body stopped him, and this time another joined it. Their arms were locked together now, and they wanted to keep him there. He looked into their eyes and saw only the smoke-dark dreamy lack of interest that was Brenda's eerie characteristic. Amanda? She was not Amanda now!

Julie? She was a creature of the Dark Ages!

'Julie!' said Jerry, croaking and trying for normalcy in his tones. 'Let me — '

'Wait!' whispered Brenda. 'Jerry — Look!'

He did not dare turn, for he knew that things spewed out of the coalscuttle, dark things that were better unseen. No power on earth could have brought him round!

Brenda moved to face him with a swift sinuous phantom-speed. She held his frightened eyes with the eerie emptiness of her own smoke-dark and staring gaze, and he felt himself once more in the trance-like state of pre-death, just as he had experienced it two days before. His senses began to spin as the girls copied Brenda's subtle movements. He saw that the brazen engravings were no longer the products of some long-dead craftsman's skill; they were not lines in ancient brass, they were the forces that had been implanted into the metal, forces which could move out and take hold of impressionable minds and mould them into elementals! And he could do nothing!

Brenda's mouth opened. White, sharp teeth, red thin lips in the yellow oil-light, but the voice was not hers. It was a dark and harsh voice, deep and confident:

'Keep away from the secret place! Do not speak of it!'

'Keep away — ' repeated Jerry, unconscious of his own feeble voice.

'Do not speak of it!' the girls whispered to him.

They writhed towards him, the closed circle of girls. He felt himself sinking into their spell, surrendering to the combined exertion of malevolence: *why struggle?* voices inside his skull whispered; and the girls' faces were triumphant. *Do as she says!*

He was about to declare himself when Bill Ainsley's voice roared from down the corridor:

'Aye, Brenda! Listen! It's the news! You're on, you lasses!'

And the spell was gone in a flash, and the girls suddenly aware of themselves as people, for Bill Ainsley had put the transistor up to full blast and they could all hear the middle of the story:

' . . . stranded for two nights now on the mountains of the Peak District. Their schoolmistress, Miss Walker-Harbottle, was extremely worried about them, but a recent report from the Mountain Rescue Centre at Edale gives us the news that all twelve girls are fit and well. Their pot-holing expedition has brought them excitement and hardships that they were not expecting! Their next-of-kin have all been informed, and we are assured that there is no immediate danger for any member of the party. And now, fresh news of riots in . . . '

'It's us!' squealed Amanda. 'Jerry, it's us!'

Julie was slower to return to the self-possessed schoolgirl she had been:

'I'm glad Butch didn't get up here,' she said, looking at Brenda. The lorry-girl smiled her snarl-smile.

'You've 'ad a bit of fun,' she said,

'Yes,' whispered Jerry.

'And there's no immediate danger,'

Julie told him. She looked at him threateningly.

'No,' Jerry said. Not immediately. That fool of a broadcaster wouldn't know. 'Bill!' he said, edging through the group listening to the rest of the news for a mention of themselves, 'can I talk to you?'

'Stay,' called Julie, as Jerry went. 'Stay and play cards.' She took hold of his sweater.

Brenda made a slight movement with her hand and Julie released the sweating young man. Jerry knew real fear again then, for Brenda was so sure of herself that she could dismiss him almost with contempt. He fled.

'Bill,' Jerry said, lying, 'Mrs. Raybould wants a word with you.'

Bill obediently followed him to the kitchen. The Raybouds were sitting morosely by the light of a dim oil-lamp watching Sukie, who in turn watched her meal. Mrs. Raybould encouraged her by offering tidbits.

'Hello, Sylv?' asked Bill.

'What do you want?' she asked, in a hostile voice.

'Nothing, love. He said you wanted me.'

'I did,' Jerry said. 'I wasn't telling the truth exactly — it was me that wanted to see you again, Bill. Listen — I've been talking to Mr. and Mrs. Raybould . . . '

'He's been talking about Sukie,' said Mrs. Raybould. 'And *her*.'

'Yes, I have! I went for the beret just now — Lord knows why, I was a bit confused myself, and they were at it again!'

'Who?' asked Bill.

'Why, all those girls — they were conjuring something up with that coalscuttle,' Jerry said to Mrs. Raybould, 'just like the time the other night when Sukie couldn't settle.'

Mrs. Raybould looked at the white poodle. 'She's off her food now.'

'Listen,' Jerry said. 'The girls and Brenda are trying to stop us going down the cellar. Don't you believe there's some bodies down there? Bill?'

Bill looked away. 'Could be.'

'I saw them! And the beret's there!'

'Then yes.'

'Mrs. Raybould?' asked Jerry.

'I don't know!' she said impatiently.

'Sam?'

'Aye, well, I went for paraffin a bit ago. Whilst you were asleep this afternoon.'

'What? You went in the tunnel? You saw them?'

'He didn't dare!' Mrs. Raybould snapped. 'I watched him go down and come up. Then I put the bolts on again!'

'So what did you see?' Jerry groaned.

Raybould pointed to a cupboard under the sink.

'In there.'

Jerry hobbled over to the cupboard. He opened it, and the scent of decaying matter came to him, a ghastly reminder of the shadowy green things that lay in the tunnel. He conquered his aversion and grasped the thing in the darkness. It was a bag of some kind, greasy and slimy with mildew, leather once but a rotting, jelly-like substance now. He held it at arm's length.

'What is it?' Bill demanded. 'A kid's satchel?'

Jerry could see where the straps had

been attached to it. And it was a leather satchel or wallet of some kind, the sort of thing that travellers carried before the rucksack was adopted; perhaps it was the size of a child's school satchel.

'It's old,' said Raybould. 'And it weren't in cellar early on before you went down.'

'The straps,' said Jerry. 'I must have picked it up whilst I was down there! Doesn't this prove it, Mrs. Raybould!'

Sukie yipped at the stinking thing. She wanted it. There was a decaying odour about it that pleased her.

'We'll have Arthur Rowbotham along when this lot's been shifted,' said Raybould, pointing to the window, piled high with snow.

Mrs. Raybould did not argue, and Jerry felt a leap of exultation. At last they believed him!

'Right!' he said. 'Now, let's see what's in it.'

He placed it on the floor. Raybould passed a knife and Jerry slit through the wet material.

He slipped his hand inside and drew

out a small stone bottle. The inside of the satchel was reasonably well preserved, for there was an inner lining of softer leather. He fished inside again, and drew out a leather-bound book. Its cover was wet and soft, and the metal lock was green and coated; but Jerry again felt a glow of triumph when he made out the marbling along the top edge of the volume.

'It's old,' said Raybould, his wet eyes inquisitive. 'Whose is it?'

'I don't know,' said Jerry. 'I'll have to break the lock. It's been down there years! I told you I thought I saw a body dressed in old-fashioned clothes — this must have been his!'

'It's best not meddled with,' Mrs Raybould said, but all three men knew that this was a ritual female statement and that they should ignore her.

Jerry took a kitchen-knife and slid the blade into the book. The knife slipped and he almost cut himself.

Bill Ainsley had a question.

'You think there's something in what you were saying about that diary?'

'Walpurgisnacht?'

'What's that?' said Raybould.

'He was saying there's always trouble at the end of April,' said Bill. 'He'd worked it all out. There was this day — '

'Night,' said Jerry. 'Saint Walpurga was a holy and well-loved medieval missionary, if a trifle impetuous. Her name is commemorated as Walpurgisnacht.'

'A saint,' said Mrs. Raybould. 'Well, then.'

'That's right. She won't bother us,' said Jerry. 'Saint Walpurga's Night had another significance in the earlier religions. It was May Day Eve. 'Yes,' he said, reading the scared look on Raybould's face, 'yes, your old villagers were right about that. You see, the Eve of May Day was one of the great festivals of the Old Religions. It was a night for sacrifices.'

'Sacrifices? How do you mean?'

'There were varying practices. The earliest would have been human victims,' said Jerry. 'What's more to the point is that the May Day Eve festivals were adopted, or rather continued, by worshippers up to recent times.'

'Who?' asked Raybould.

'Your local Satanists,' said Jerry. 'Bad Lord Titus. Walpurgisnacht is the night the Devil attends his Grand Sabbat.'

'May Day Eve?' asked Bill Ainsley, and Jerry could see that he was sweating.

'Yes.'

'And that's — '

'Tonight.'

11

There was a rush of questions from the Rayboulds and Bill Ainsley, and Jerry had the heady pleasure of providing information.

'As I see it, there's three distinct elements in the situation. First, there's the legend. The tale of the Brindleys being carried into Hag Hole. Mr. Raybould, is that all you know of the Brindleys? Have you heard anything else?'

'I told you all as I 'eard. There's Mrs. Starkie, who's over ninety, as knows all about the tales — she says Lord Titus went out with all of 'is relatives and they danced themselves right into the 'Ole — the lot gone, just like that! Every last one on 'em, father, son — '

' — and Grandfather Brindley with the beast's foot,' said Jerry. 'He'd have a club foot, or maybe he was born with six toes or webbed feet. There'd be a reason for

179

the detail — there's always truth some-where. And that's all?'

'Devil took 'em!'

'Old wives' tale,' said Mrs. Raybould, without conviction. 'He goes boozing and comes back talking a load of rubbish.'

'You said it was all rubbish too,' Bill Ainsley said.

'So I did,' said Jerry. 'But I hadn't seen what Brenda was up to. Not then. She's the second strand. Bill, doesn't it strike you that she's always around when there's some nasty business?'

Bill shrugged. 'She's just a slag.'

'She's all of that!' Mrs. Raybould snorted. 'And you encouraging her!'

'Let's keep calm, shall we?' ordered Jerry. 'Now, Mr. Raybould, what do you make of that coalscuttle? It came from the cellars, you say?'

'Aye. When we were clearing out the rubble, it were dug up. It's been lying around years. I only brought it up this summer.'

'And Brenda likes it — she's always stroking it,' said Jerry. 'Don't you see, something about the engravings has

180

something to do with the other thing?'

'What other thing?' asked Bill.

'Why, Lord Titus and his club foot!' Jerry said. 'And now things start to happen again, just when Brenda's here! There's always been the Walpurgisnacht element — the bomber coming down, the Boy Scouts getting lost, the lieutenant losing his way. Always on May Day Eve!'

'And you saw the bodies down there,' said Bill Ainsley. He pointed towards the cellar. 'You reckon Brenda's been in the tunnel?'

'No,' said Jerry. 'But we know she wants to.'

'How?'

Jerry realised that he hadn't told Bill Ainsley of Brenda's excursion with Sam Raybould. Mrs. Raybould was stonily silent, so it was left to her husband to explain.

'She saw the cellar,' said Raybould. 'I sent her to get coal.'

'Coal!' spat Mrs. Raybould. 'It wasn't coal she was after!'

'Oh,' Bill said. It was clear that he understood.

'While you were out at lorry,' Raybould added.

'So she went down,' said Bill Ainsley. 'You reckon she's after something?'

'I'm glad I don't know,' said Jerry seriously. 'The three things go together: this eighteenth-century Satanist, Lord Titus Brindley; Brenda and what *she's* up to; and those poor creatures who ended up in Hag Hole.'

'So what do you make of it all?' asked Bill.

'Nothing!' said Mrs. Raybould. 'Just a parcel of silly lasses! No one goes down there! Not till the thaw comes!'

'I couldn't agree more,' said Jerry. 'The safest thing we can do is to stay together until all this is over, and keep well away from the cellar.'

'You must have your own notion of what it's all about,' persisted Bill.

'I'd be guessing,' said Jerry. 'I'd want some evidence before committing myself.' His fingers shook as he picked up the old volume. 'This is evidence.'

'It's only an old book,' said Mrs. Raybould.

'It's more,' said Jerry, slitting through the rotting leather, so that the corroded hasp fell away. 'It's some sort of journal.'

With growing excitement, he turned to the flyleaf. The paper was damp, but it had not yet begun to pulp. The writing was neat, large and elaborate, an educated man's copperplate hand; the ink had run, but not much.

''Alfred Douglas Davenant,' Jerry read aloud. ''Gentleman and Antiquarist.' It's his journal! *Antiquarist!*' he said impatiently, looking up to see the bewilderment of the others. 'That's the nineteenth century term for archaeologist and historian! And a confounded nuisance they were! They broke into barrows and destroyed important things — they were only treasure-seekers really! Usually country squires who'd read a bit about the finding of Pompeii and hoped for a few bits of gold, or a statue for the garden!'

'Gold?' said Raybould.

'What does it say?' asked Bill Ainsley.

'Don't interrupt,' said Jerry abstractedly. 'It's not easy. The damp's blurred the ink right through — but it's certainly a diary. See! He found unmarked pages and turned the mouldly pages back. ''The Twenty-Eighth Day of April, 1827' — that's the most recent entry. He turned more pages back. 'Here, see!' Jerry said, pointing to the stained page he had read from. 'Look — ' so I duly paid the woman for her trouble and set off to inquire into this bizarre tale, and in truth I must confess that I was in need of some diversion in consequence of the melancholia which had afflicted me since the death of my beloved Louisa . . . ' Louisa? His wife, I suppose. Can't he get to the point! Here! It's mentioned! ' . . . it seems that there is a great Pit in the side of the mountain so that mine ancient informant's story in this regard has all the appearances of accuracy. How will the rest of the wonders she has told me, and which she so earnestly believes in, I am fully convinced, hold good once I betake myself inside this extraordinary manifestatIon of Nature?' It's Hag Hole! It must be! Bill, I'll have to read back a few pages!'

He settled down to read the old-fashioned script, tracing the events recorded in the diary. Raybould muttered complaints from time to time, mostly about the schoolgirls. He wandered off quite soon, but Jerry did not notice him leave. At length, as Jerry remained silent, Bill Ainsley became bored and he too left the kitchen. But Mrs. Raybould stayed. She made fresh tea for the little white poodle; Jerry accepted a cup as well with no more than a grunt of acknowledgement. He felt his head bursting with amazed pride as He read on and found the information that would make a coherent whole of the slender clues and half-truths he had heard. Alfred Douglas Davenant had been more than a gentleman-forager. He had been a meticulous scholar who had tracked down the source of the legend of Hag Hole!

Jerry looked up:

'My God, it's all here, Mrs. Raybould! Do you know what you've been living over for the past twenty years?'

She administered to Sukie, not looking at him. 'It's best left to them as is paid for it!'

Jerry looked down again, fingering the flowing script with the devotion of a scholar.

'Jerry!' called Bill Ainsley from the passage. 'Jerry, lad, for God's sake!'

He stumbled in, face ashen. Whatever had occurred had been enough to shake him out of his dull acceptance of life. But Jerry had his own news:

'I've discovered the connection between the Castle and Hag Hole, Bill! It was the Brindleys!'

'Jerry, I've seen them!' Bill Ainsley gasped. 'She's in it — I'd have wrung her neck if I'd dared, but I couldn't go near her!' He shuddered with revulsion. 'Lad, I'd not dare go near any of them now!'

Jerry frowned. 'Is there some tea for him, Mrs. Raybould?'

'Why, what's he seen?'

Jerry took the teapot, for Mrs. Raybould still nursed a grudge against the amorous driver.

'Christ!' Bill said. 'It's tonight! It's to

be tonight! What time is it?'

'A quarter past ten,' said Mrs. Raybould. 'Mind that tea. Sukie-darling wants another saucer.'

'What were they doing, Bill?' Jerry asked.

Bill gasped for breath. Mrs. Raybould poured milk into his tea and pushed it at him. When he had drunk deeply, he said:

'I couldn't believe it, Jerry. They're all undressed in there — Brenda and every last one of them! And she's had something boiling up on the fire in that coalscuttle, and it stinks something cruel! Some sort of fat or grease, but there's another smell, I don't know what it'll be — '

'I can guess!' said Jerry. 'My God, Alfred Douglas knew what he was about!'

'She was throwing bits of grass or roots — and dried berries — from her bag into the scuttle, and they were all moaning together, as if they'd gone mad! I was going to ask them what they were up to, but I thought I'd better not, them being undressed. And I wanted to laugh at first, till I saw what they were making!'

'Making?' said Mrs. Raybould. 'Them lasses?'

'Yes! Christ, I couldn't believe it! Jerry, you know the blonde lass?'

'Julie — she was carrying a wool teddy bear.'

'They'd torn the head off, and they were stitching it up! They'd sewn the face up — and there's horns and a beard on it, and they'd got it fastened to some broken chair legs — '

'My chairs!' said Mrs. Raybould. She got to her feet.

'No!' said Jerry, 'if you value your sanity — or your soul — don't go! We can't stop them, no one can. All we can do is keep ourselves out of danger! Look what happened to everyone who went near the cavern on Walpurgisnacht! No, Mrs. Raybould!'

She sat down as both he and Bill put a hand on her shoulders.

'Why?' she said, thoroughly frightened. 'What's going on!'

Sukie stopped drinking tea and cringed beside her, whimpering with fear.

'She's every right to be frightened,' said

Jerry. 'If Bill's seen what I think he's seen, then the girls are beyond human help at the moment.'

'Why?' said Mrs. Raybould.

'They're preparing for the Grand Sabbat! What Bill saw just now was the ritual goat's mask, and the chair legs he saw will be for the mock-altar.

'Mock-altar,' said Bill Ainsley. 'What for?'

'The Black Mass,' said Jerry grimly. He pointed to the old journal. 'It was the ceremony used in devil-worship. Davenant records some of the practices used in black magic.'

'But what are they up to?' Mrs. Raybould said. 'I know they were on about the cellar and you said — '

She stopped.

'The Brindleys,' said Jerry, recognising that she too now accepted the truth. 'It all hangs together now. Walpurgisnacht is the night when the Brindleys can use their power. And my God how they've used it!'

'Then what's that stuff they're boiling up?' asked Bill.

'Had they got their first-aid tins out?'

'Aye, but — '

'Grease,' said Jerry. 'They'll rub themselves with it. Alfred Douglas has something about it.' He opened the ancient journal. 'Listen: 'I have it on good authority that the Brindleys resorted to all the potions available to less enlightened times, and that they were not averse to the use of Aconitum and even Belladonna in order to bring on those delirious frenzies which, so they believed, made them able to enter into a fitting state for communion with their Master' . . . '

'But what's it all for?' Bill said. 'What's this got to do with the Brindleys? And what's in that, anyway?' he said, pointing to the journal.

'I'll explain — briefly! Sam was right about the Brindleys; the local legend is true. They were the local aristocracy about two hundred years ago, and they were black magicians — Satanists, though they'd call themselves Followers of the Old Religion, I expect. Anyway, they must have had some sort of Sabbat — that's what the legend meant when it declared that they'd gone into Hag Hole. They

190

would have gone there, because it's a peculiarly suitable place for religious ceremonies that have to be secret. It's underground, and if Alfred Douglas is any guide, it's got a most appropriate meeting-chamber! With me?'

'Just about,' said Bill.

'Sukie-darling eat her Doggy Delight,' Mrs. Raybould encouraged. She had cut herself off once more.

'So they went down into Hag Hole — all the Brindleys. There'd be enough for a coven — thirteen, probably, with grandfather Lord Titus as the Magister — the boss-witch. They'd be calling Satan down, perhaps to ask for favours, possibly just to keep on good terms with him. The whole family would be in it — nephews, sons, grandsons.'

Bill growled. 'Are we in any danger?'

'Probably more than we realise! If we can keep together till after midnight, though, we should be all right. There's a thaw on the way, so we'll be able to get away early tomorrow. Tonight's the difficulty.'

'Aye, but hold on a minute, Jerry,' Bill

191

frowned. 'These Brindleys — they went down Hag Hole. Then what?'

'Then nothing! Bill, they're still there! Listen: 'Being of a curious disposition, and having nothing of moment to detain me at my Manchester home, I determined on finding out the history of this singular key. The letter which had come with it, and which was almost indecipherable, due to the effects of long storage in damp conditions, was quite mysterious. It purported to be a missive from a lady's maid, and the effect of the letter was to proffer an apology for abstracting the key from the lady's desk at some time in the past, when the writer had been in the employ of the lady in question. So, a veritable mystery! Here I had a key for which there was no door, and a letter addressed to a lady whose name I did not know' . . . ' Jerry stopped, eyes gleaming. 'The old boy was brilliant — '

'Old boy? Him with this?' said Bill, indicating the satchel and the journal.

'Yes! He says he was old, he'd lost his wife, and he'd come across a mystery! I don't know why he pegged out down in the cavern — perhaps he had a heart attack, but anyway that doesn't matter now. What does matter is that we know what happened to the Brindleys!'

'What did happen, then?'

'Why, man, they went down to hold their Sabbat and they stayed down there! The door I found leads to some sort of underground chamber where they'd held their meetings! They'd made a passage-way from the cellars to Hag Hole! They'd go through the cellars down there,' said Jerry, indicating the corridor that led to the cellar door. 'Down they went through the passageway we saw! Then they'd unlock the door they'd set into the entrance to the cavern. I suppose some of the servants would get a whiff of what was happening, then the story would come out in a garbled form, with enough of substance in it for the legend to begin to grow!'

'And this Davenant got on to the story?'

'It's here!' said Jerry, pointing to the journal. 'He bought an old bureau that came from Derbyshire, and there was a letter — and a key in a secret drawer. Then he traced the letter to the High Peak and he started asking about local legends. Eventually, he heard about the Brindleys — '

'And they're down there!' Bill exclaimed.

'Yes. And there's a key to the door I told you about! The one they tried to cut their way through those Boy Scouts! The one with teeth marks!'

'There's a keyhole?'

'Yes! That's what the key's all about! It's my guess that they went to hold their Sabbat over two hundred years ago, and that they were accidentally locked into the cavern!' An unpleasant thought struck him. 'Or maybe it wasn't an accident.'

'Someone — '

'Might have locked them in. Yes!'

'Christ!' whispered Bill. 'Then what's all that about?'

He and Jerry looked towards the corridor. They could hear the sound of women's voices, not girlish high-pitched educated noises, but a low and mysterious crooning; the menace was there again, just as it had been the night before.

There was a wildness about the sound that caused Jerry's scalp and beard an uncomfortable, cold itching sensation.

'You know, don't you?' said Jerry.

'The Brindleys?'

'Yes. Walpurgisnacht, Bill. The night of power. They'll try to get the Brindleys out. That's the reason for it all. Bill, we can do nothing but stay together. And hope.'

'Try to get them out!'

'Yes. The coalscuttle is the old cauldron used by the Brindley Coven. The Power has gone into the girls.'

'A cauldron? That's a cooking pot — '

'Yes. Brenda's brewing up some sort of ointment to get them into a trance! Oh, you can find the stuff easily enough! Berries and roots — deadly nightshade, Bill! She'd have it in her duffel bag!'

'Brenda? *Brenda!*'

'She's their leader!'

'Yes, but how did she — '

'I don't know!' Jerry snapped. 'All I do know is that they'll make for the cellar!'

Mrs. Raybould talked in low tones to Sukie.

'They'll want the key Alfred Douglas Davenent came across in the bureau he bought,' said Jerry

'This key!' Bill's eyes gleamed. He was curious and afraid. 'He'd have it with him?'

'Of course. He was a brave man. He'd have wanted to find out what lay behind the door.'

Jerry saw the direction of Bill's intent look. He too found himself staring at the rotting leather satchel.

Mrs. Raybould looked up:

'Sam took it.'

Both men stared at the gaunt woman.

'I talked about treasure hunters! He *let* me go down! He must have heard something about the cavern! I said something about gold!'

Mrs. Raybould stroked Sukie:

'He never had much sense, Sam Raybould.'

The low moaning and crooning from the dining room suddenly built up into a burst of noise; Sukie put her thin neck back and howled mournfully. Then she bit Mrs. Raybould in the chin and fled.

196

'Sukie!' screamed the woman. 'Sukie-darling!'

The noise from the dining room ceased, and Mrs. Raybould came back.

'Sukie's in with them,' she said in a scared voice.

'We've more to worry about, Mrs. Raybould!' Bill growled. 'What about your Sam?'

Another sound floated down the corridor as someone opened the door to the dining room: it was the voice of the adenoidal Manchester announcer:

'And now, a special request for the twelve girls high up there in the lonesome High Peak! For the dozen beauties from Langdene Academy up in the transport café on Devil's Peak, a little number called 'That Old Black Magic'. Ha-ha-ha!'

There was an echoing bray of laughter from Brenda, a mocking and menacing flood of noise. Jerry felt his bones turn to water. It was like being on Toller Edge again. There was need for action, but he had no confidence.

'What about Sam?'

12

The transistor was switched off abruptly, and the crooning sounds began again. Words filtered through to them, quiet and insidious words that were ghosts in themselves: '*We come! The Power is on us!*' And still the girls' voices came to them, with another, harsher voice. Jerry shuddered. Could those brutal tones be manufactured by that thin throat? How could the deep, harsh, and baying noise be projected from the whippet-like body of the lorry-girl?

'Brenda!' said Bill Ainsley. 'It doesn't sound like her at all! Christ, Jerry, what are they doing — '

'The drugs are working. They'll dance — writhe — get themselves into a delirium! It's all here — Davenant has even noted the ingredients for the devil's brew!'

Bill looked at Mrs. Raybould:

'We could try for my lorry — the battery would work a heater. There'd be enough juice to keep us warm through the night. And tomorrow there's a thaw!'

'Sam,' the woman whispered. 'He's down there!'

'What time is it?' asked Jerry.

'Eleven,' said Bill Ainsley.

'An hour to go!'

Mrs. Raybould started for the door:

'Sukie-Sukie!' she moaned. 'Come to Mummy!' She turned to Jerry: 'You go and get her! It's all your fault! If you hadn't got caught in the snow, she wouldn't be here! Go and get Sukie!'

Jerry knew it was more than his soul could bear. 'Yes, yes, all right!' he lied.

'Go and sort them lasses out! They're just a lot of schoolgirls playing games!' the woman insisted. 'Go *on*!'

'What do you mean, an hour?' asked Bill Ainsley, ignoring the woman's distress.

'That's the time of the Grand Sabbat! It's the most potent time for the satanic forces — remember the Nazi bomber! It was caught in a beam on May Day Eve

— and that must have been about midnight!'

'I don't care about that,' said Mrs. Raybould. 'You get Sukie in here! And tell those lasses to go to bed!'

Jerry went to the door and turned back as the noise from the dining room built up once more.

'I daren't!' Jerry shuddered. Nor Bill, and I don't advise you to! There's something happening in there that's beyond human comprehension. If you go in to them, you'll be in the most ghastly danger! Those things they're using are only the symbols of something that is terrifyingly dangerous! Don't you realise, Mrs. Raybould, that those young girls are attempting to carry out experiments that have not been tried on this Earth for two hundred years or more?'

'I don't want any part of it,' said Bill Ainsley. 'How about my lorry?'

'How about Sukie!'

'Mrs. Raybould,' said Jerry quietly, after his impassioned outburst. 'Am I getting through to you?'

'I suppose so.'

'They intend,' Jerry said quietly, 'to raise Satan Himself.'

Bill Ainsley regarded Jerry with a deferential watchfulness in his eyes. Jerry knew that he was being assessed.

Bill spoke at last:

'What about Sam Raybould?'

Jerry looked down at the journal. Alfred Douglas Davenant had known what to do. It was all there: he was a man of almost sixty years who had been widowed after a happy married life. Childless, without occupation, he had been obsessed with the strange shreds of past events that had come his way; and he had ventured into the bowels of the earth to face the Adversary. He had, in his own words, braved 'The Venomous Serpent'. There they were, the words of the Prayer for Relief from Diabolic Inhabitation: 'Deliver this Thy servant from Unclean Spirits and from the Worm that dieth not. He who cast out the sorcerers with a mist and Darkness commands the Vile affliction of Mankind to flee, for He shall Burn up his Enemies with a Sword of Fire, and destroy the

Venomous Serpent in its Flames.' And he had died, his key still in the satchel.

'Sam?' asked Bill Ainsley.

More frightened, more confused than he had ever been in his life, Jerry heard the words coming from, his own mouth and marvelled at them. 'We'll get him out,' he was saying. 'They'll be dancing themselves into an hypnotic trance now — we've more than half an hour, that's plenty of time to go down and get Sam. Then we'll make for your tanker, Bill. That's what we'll do!'

Bill Ainsley, ex-soldier that he was, recognised the authentic tones of the lower middle-class officers he used to obey.

'Right!'

Mrs. Raybould looked her astonishment.

'You're not to go down the cellar!'

'We are!' snapped Jerry back. 'Get the lamp, Bill!'

He grinned at Bill Ainsley, then groaned as he put weight on his gammy leg. Bill opened the kitchen door, and the noise from the dining room now had an animal quality about it: Brenda spoke out in her usual grating tones, then a change came, and what the two men heard was a ringing, iron voice full of impatience: 'Soon! Soon, Magister!'

'You first!' snapped Jerry, forcing the words out.

They came to the cellar door, and he took a step back, but the cursed mood of arrogant terror still held him, and he followed the unimaginative Bill Ainsley into the darkness, with only one oil lamp to light the vast and gloomy archways of the cellar.

'Lights,' said Bill. 'I'll get some torches from the boxes — that do?'

'Yes!'

'Here, one each,' breathed Bill. 'Shall I leave the lamp?'

They faced the fallen masonry and the tunnel beyond. The steady yellow light of the oil-lamp was supplemented by the harsh brilliance of Bill's big electric torch, which played on the walls and roof and showed up the pick marks of two hundred years ago; it showed too the centre of darkness beyond, where the tunnel curved away and joined the natural underground roadway carved out so long ago by the force of enormous water pressure.

'Yes, leave the oil-lamp. Come on, I'll go first,' Jerry said.

'Twenty to twelve,' said Bill Ainsley nervously.

'Then let's go.'

Jerry limped ahead, careful on the jumbled bricks and wet mortar. The floor of the tunnel was wet, with a small stream running along one side; overhead there was a steady drip of water. Drops caught his neck, increasing the ice-like terror that encased him. The turning came too soon, it was only two minutes' walk, even at the slow pace Jerry was forced to use.

They turned the corner. Jerry forced his nerveless hand and wrist to move the heavy Mountain Rescue torch towards the door he had glimpsed once before. It played instead on the long, silent, ghastly-green figure splayed out in the tunnel floor.

'Oh, Christ!' Bill Ainsley shuddered. 'Dear God, lad, it's the Signals lieutenant!

There's his tool-case!'

Jerry had not noticed it before, but there was a webbed canvas satchel just beyond the pitiful corpse. 'See!' he whispered, playing the beam of the torch towards the door. Then it was his turn to call out in horror and move involuntarily backwards, 'My God, Bill! It's Sam Raybould!'

The light of the two beams shook, and Bill Ainsley cursed softly under his breath.

'Sam!' yelled Jerry, heedless of danger. 'Sam!'

The door was partly open, and Raybould was propped up, eyes staring and wide open, as if caught trying to escape from the scenes he had witnessed.

'He's dead!' Bill Ainsley said hoarsely. 'Dead — Jerry, there's another!' He had seen the other rotting corpses now. 'Dear God, more! It's the missing Scouts — two of them!'

'Sam isn't dead,' said Jerry. He moved forward, controlling his shivering so that he could keep the torch on the scrunched-up features of Raybould. 'No — he's petrified, but he isn't dead!'

'He is — leave him! Let's get back!'

'No!'

Jerry could see into the part-open door, but he would not admit that there was anything beyond; to do so would be to allow the thousand terrors of Castle Café and all its midnight horrors to take possession of his spirit.

'It's a quarter to midnight!'

'Help me!'

Jerry limped towards Sam Raybould. The man was breathing, though with such shallow movements that Bill could be forgiven for thinking him dead; his face was dead-white, his jaw hung slackly, and he would have fallen but for the fact that he was caught on the massive and ornate key in the half-open door. Jerry and Bill Ainsley reached the door together, and Jerry saw that the café-owner was suspended by his braces, otherwise he would have joined the other victims of Hag Hole on the cold floor.

Raybould's eyes were still open. Though there was a reflex action of evasion as Jerry shone his powerful torch into the man's face, he was paralysed, quite lax as if asleep. He could do nothing for himself, though Bill Ainsley tried:

'Sam! Can you walk! Sam! Christ, Sam, you'd best be stirring! He can't!' Bill said, turning for guidance to Jerry.

'Can you carry him?'

'Aye.'

'Then get him!'

Bill reached for the thin body. He struggled with the braces, whilst Jerry held both torches. Then, as the limp body came free, the door swung wide open, so that the interior was revealed. Raybould slipped through Bill Ainsley's fingers:

'No,' shuddered the lorry-driver, as the light from two heavy-duty torches, manufactured especially to penetrate the murk of Pennine mists, shed a cold brilliance through the doorway.

Jerry was rooted to the spot.

There was a cavern, a natural rock chamber that had been eaten from the limestone in some continuous scouring process hundreds of thousands of years' before. It was perhaps a hundred feet deep, and almost as wide as its length; in tiny sub-caves hung stalactites, joined, in some cases, to stalagmites. At the back of the cavern was a clump of such rock columns, formed by the tiny accretions of rock through thousands of years of deposits by the water that dripped from the roof. It was not the natural glories of the place, however, that blasted the men's senses, making them stand, reeling; the shock that had brought Raybould to a complete physical collapse was almost as severe to Jerry and Bill Ainsley; for, seated at a long table, still upright after two long centuries of incarceration, were the frozen bodies of the Brindley Coven!

Their faces were stilt faces, their hands, some resting on the table, some propping up long, intelligent chins were still hands; a green fluorescent radiance came from faces and hands as if metallic fires glowed beneath the skin. There were young and old men, but all gaunt, withered, dried up; they were a ghastly feasting-party in their rotten coats and shredded trousers. Jerry would have retreated, but he could not move. Bill Ainsley's jaw worked, but no sound came. They stared in horror at the silent assembly, especially at the figure that headed the long, narrow table: angular, thin, upright, snow-haired, with heavy bushy eyebrows, eyes wide open and black as pitch, and a faint sneer on the cruel mouth that exposed fang-like teeth.

Jerry found his voice:

'Brindley!' he shuddered.

The antique clothes were bright green with mildew, but they glowed too with the eerie radiance that shone from the flesh; here and there, Jerry could make out a once-bright thread of green gold in the fabrics. They were all so monstrously at ease, these long-dead corpses sat to wait —

Jerry moved now. He turned the torch. There was more. He saw that on the table were cups and dishes; the Brindleys had been about to feast. It was indeed a most terrible birthday party! When he could look around the great cavern, Jerry distinguished a canopy set out behind the chair where Lord Titus sat. In it, green and awful, was the ruin of a terrible altar. There was a cross of a sort, though a perverted mockery of a thing: on it, some animal was nailed, for the skull still snarled with curved fangs, and hair clung to the bones of the neck. There was a chalice too; jugs, and candlesticks. In some, still upright, were what might have been candles.

'He was right!' whispered Jerry. 'Arthur Douglas Davenant had got it right, down to the last detail! The whole Devil's crew! Just as they were when the key was turned.'

'Jerry,' whispered Bill Ainsley, and he was now deathly afraid. 'They're all dead?'

'Dead as mutton!' said Jerry, still shuddering, but able now to master his complete terror.

'I thought he — '

'Lord Titus? What?'

' — moved!'

Some vibration of the air reached the ancient altar, and even that slight movement was enough to make the slimy wood give way; for slowly and with a sickening splash, the goat's head, the altar, the dreadful appurtenances of the Black Mass, gave way. The two men did not dare to move.

'Dear Christ!' whispered Jerry. 'She knew they would need a new altar! She *knew*!'

'Then these lasses — ' began Bill.

'They'll be down!' Jerry said, suddenly remembering the schoolgirls and the enigmatic figure who led them. 'Get Sam — '

'Yes!'

Bill slung the slack body over his shoulder, and both men hurried towards the cellar. Behind them, the door hung open; Jerry stumbled after Bill Ainsley with the fear of spiritual extinction at his neck. He fancied he could hear tremors, dragging footsteps, faint creaking sounds as ancient cloth unfolded and long-dead limbs were activated. Once, he shone his torch back and saw nothing but the green radiance from the open doorway. Bill hurried on, though he was careful to avoid crashing Raybould's slack body into the sides of the tunnel. They reached the turning and, blessedly, the man-made connecting tunnel that led to the cellar. And there was the familiar and homely light of the oil-lamp.

'Thank God!' Bill called, in something like his normal voice. He stooped. 'The lamp — can you get it?'

'Leave it!' Jerry said. 'Let's get out of here — it must be nearly midnight!'

Bill Ainsley looked at his watch.

'Ten to.'

'Then come on!' he ordered. 'Bill!'

Bill stared back at the ragged mouth of the tunnel. 'We can't let those schoolgirls go down there!'

'No,' shuddered Jerry. 'They're not — they're possessed! Their souls aren't their own tonight.'

'And there's Brenda!'

Jerry understood. The recent liaison meant something to the lorry-driver.

'No! She's one of them! A Brindley! That mark on her back — that's the Devil's mark! Davenant records it in his journal! All the Brindleys have a Devil's mark, Bill! Now, for Christ's sake let's go!'

But Bill had recovered himself; he was no longer the trusty NCO; he was bloody-minded Bill Ainsley, who did what he thought was right.

'Brenda's just a daft young slag! I can't have her going in there! I'm blocking it up! Give me a hand with the boxes!' he ordered, pointing to the Rescue gear. 'Block the tunnel up! They'll not be able to find it and get in!'

He deposited Raybould roughly and hefted one of the five-foot long boxes towards the detritus and rubble at the tunnel mouth. Then he had two boxes in position, hiding part of the tunnel.

Jerry was almost convinced by his reasoning, but he could hear now the low and insistent noises from the dining room.

'Let's take Sam up!'

But Bill's bull-strength and ignorant will prevailed, and Jerry found himself heaving on yet another box, this one open. Its contents spilled out as Bill Ainsley used his broad back to get it into position.

'One more!' he grunted.

He stopped, for there was a rush of sound above. There was a light, increasing in strength, at the cellar door. Women's voices, hypnotic, low and wild, began to chant:

'*Magister, we come! The Power is on us, and the Hour is now!*'

'Bill! They're here!'

'I'll go up and talk — '

'No! Get Sam!'

The sounds were closer, and the iron voice that was Brenda's and something else's, rang out in dull and menacing tones:

'*His Power is in us! We feel it, Magister!*'

There was a Power suddenly in the ancient, dank cellar. There was a feeling of an alien presence, a brooding quietness that was coiled, expectant, hopeful.

'Jerry!' Bill Ainsley croaked, and Jerry could hear the torment in the lorry-driver's tones.

'We can't go back up there now,' Jerry whispered, the evil spell broken by the sound of a human voice. 'Get the boxes away! Quick! And grab Sam!'

Jerry attacked the stack of boxes, sending them down with Bill Ainsley's help. The noises from above were infinitely strange now, harsh and terrible. And the words were strange! Latin? No! Older?

Sam Raybould startled them both by groaning miserably.

'Come on, Sam!' Bill Ainsley urged, but the café-owner was still in his paralysed state.

'Right — the torches!' Jerry said, but the powerful electric torches had been placed on the stairs to provide light for the stacking of the boxes. He grabbed the oil-lamp in an unsteady hand and left the torches burning; not for anything would he approach the cellar stairs!

He pushed the last box aside and let Bill Ainsley go ahead; as the opened box slid away, Jerry had the sense to rummage inside it for another torch; his hand came into contact with a number of long tubes but no torch. Candles? He grabbed without looking and lit the way for the burdened lorry-driver. They came to the turning.

'Christ!' Bill Ainsley swore loudly as they saw the open door.

'Go on!'

There was horror ahead, the ghastly mausoleum of the Brindleys, the pathetic remnants of the victims of Hag Hole; but there was worse behind!

'Right! Wake up, Sam!' urged Bill Ainsley.

There was a thin, gurgling sound, and the café-owner returned from his empty existence. 'Don't go in there!' Raybould croaked, as they neared the entrance to the great cavern. 'I'm all right, Bill!'

Bill Ainsley stopped and lowered the café-owner. 'I'll take the oil-lamp!' he said to Jerry. 'Which way?'

Jerry pointed to the tunnel sloping downwards. 'There! God knows where it leads to, but anything's preferable to them!'

Raybould was shaky on his feet. 'Why! Let's go upstairs!'

'No!' Bill Ainsley said. He shook the man's thin shoulder. 'We can't — they're coming down!'

'They're possessed, Mr. Raybould!' Jerry said. 'When they get down here, they'll hold a Grand Sabbat! A Black Mass!'

Raybould stared from one to another. 'It's beyond me!'

'And me!' said Jerry. 'It must be nearly midnight!'

'We're best out of it!' Bill grunted, leading the way.

'Where's Sylv?' Raybould asked, when they had gone a few paces. They were standing near the decayed corpse of Alfred Douglas, but they were in such a state of hypnotised terror that one more corpse could do little to intensify their condition.

'She's in the kitchen!' said Jerry. 'She'll be all right — they're not interested in the living!'

'Come on, then,' said Raybould. He didn't ask any more questions.

Bill began to hurry away, but an idea of such overpowering wonder burst on Jerry that he stopped.

'I'll be along!' Jerry called. 'I'll lock the door!'

He turned back, took four paces, reached the open door and stumbled on the webbing satchel of the dead Army officer. Bill Ainsley called to him, but his shout was lost in a burst of exultant yelling from the cellar.

Jerry tried to get to his feet. Light streamed from the turning which led to the cellar; he could hear voices as he slithered in the detritus beneath him; he slipped on his sprained ankle and bit back the shout that almost forced its way out.

'Come on!' Bill called hoarsely.

'Leave him!' Raybould urged.

Jerry tried again, desperately, and got to one knee. Brenda's voice was heavy, iron, eager.

The girls were coming around the corner. Jerry could not escape.

The open doorway was darkly ahead.

He slithered through it, made towards the right and, remembering a tiny side-cave with a row of stalagmites half-hiding its entrance, gasped and crawled in a sea of pain and terror towards it.

A burst of chanting rang about the cave. Light was flung to every corner.

The entire frightful scene was unveiled.

Jerry looked and saw that the naked, chanting, terrible girls were each carrying a burden. Two of them held a strange cross to which was nailed the awful toy

— transmuted now into a goat's head that leered from glass eyes with an uncanny brilliance further heightened by the green of the cavern. Two more carried the still-smoking great brazen cauldron. Jerry caught the acrid whiff of herbs and the sickly stench of melted Vaseline. He choked back an urge to cough. And still more of the no-longer schoolgirls entered! Some had oil-lamps, others candles which had been smeared with chimney-soot to blacken them. He picked out the whippet-body of Brenda. The red mark on her spine seemed to jump at her back. She alone had both hands free.

He shuddered.

Julie had a basket, and in it something whimpered softly.

13

Jerry forced his cold body deeper into the shadowy recess. There were small pools of icy water, but he scarcely noticed them; behind the small screen of stalactites and stalagmites he was hidden from sight. If he kept still, the fearful girls might not see him!

For a few seconds, whilst the girls assembled in the great cavern, Jerry tried to tell himself that this could not be happening to him.

The stink of the melted oil, the fumes from the herbs, the vibration of the air as the girls chanted in those low, harsh voices, and the low whining from the basket which Julie was placing by the ancient canopy that lay behind the dehydrated corpse of Lord Titus Brindley, all combined to destroy the comfort of those few seconds. This was no charade.

It was real, evilly real, brutally evil! There was a strength of purpose about the lorry-girl and her willing acolytes that spoke of a great and malevolent design. Jerry could see the resolve in the girl's eyes.

The chanting stopped.

The wild, ancient words were only echoes now, drifting upwards to lose themselves in the brilliant clusters of spear-like stalactites in the roof of the great cavern.

How in God's name did they know the procedures of the Grand Sabbat? Jerry struggled with disbelief.

Then the fascination of the scene gripped him: he was a witness of the most fearful of all ceremonies, the deliberate and solemn undertaking to raise the Power of Evil in the person of Satan Himself! Everything was being done in its due order. It was all as Davenant had discovered!

What next?

Davenant had spoken of a trance-like state induced by the Aconitum and Belladonna. Well, that was most effectively under way. These young girls were automatons, no longer in control of their

221

senses, no longer free agents; they had writhed and chanted, just as Brenda had taught them the night before, it had been a rehearsal, he could see that now. But for what?

Jerry could feel the journal in his anorak pocket. He couldn't recall the next stage of the ceremony as the Rector had portrayed it. But there was something about a hand. A bright hand? A light hand? Whose hand? Brenda's?

He sensed the thrill of urgency in the eerie scene; Brenda stood before the stone slab in silence. She indicated the disintegrating heap of wet, rotted wood and detritus that had been the Brindleys' altar to Satan. Amanda and two of the others swiftly scooped the pile of debris away. Jerry gulped as Julie moved forward to place the basket near the new altar. Whatever was in the basket was silent by this time. Brenda supervised the establishment of the rough and ready shrine. She motioned to Amanda to fix the cross to a socket in the stone base of the former altar; then she made sure that the evil goat's head faced the silent dead company.

Another girl came forward, eager and stone-eyed, with two of Mrs. Raybould's emergency supply of candles; the white wax had been blackened. Amanda took them. Carefully but quickly she placed them in position on either side of the grinning head. More candles were brought as the ancient green candlesticks were cleaned out, and soon there were two dozen or more of the soot-grimed candles in position. There was such efficiency in the girls' actions that they looked like some band of robotic servitors; lax-limbed, but supremely confident, the schoolgirls might have been doing these tasks for years. It had taken only a few minutes for the entire scene to be transformed.

Brenda motioned to another girl who came forward with her duffel bag. Brenda reached out and produced a thin candle, more a taper, long and rough-shaped.

Julie came forward to light it with the oil-lamp. It threw off a dense, sulphurous smoke. With this crude taper the lorry-girl moved sinuously about the altar. First she lit the candles on either side of the devil-mask that had once been Julie's teddy bear; the candles flickered twice and then burned brightly, illuminating the terrible symbol of evil with a yellow-white radiance. Then Brenda moved on to light the other candles, until they all flared upwards, flames shivering occasionally as a chance motion of air disturbed them. But there were more rough, homemade tapers, Jerry saw.

Brenda smiled at one of the hypnotised servitors, and the girl smiled back. She turned from the fearful altar and ran past the long table, with its verdigris-encrusted drinking cups, its bowls of long-rotted food, and its silent double row of green long-dead. The girl brushed past an ancient sleeve, and Jerry distinctly saw a patch of material fall away to disclose an emaciated shoulder. He felt sick. Again he had the sensation that this was something he was dreaming. Then a small cracking sound from the tunnel behind him helped him recover his wits. He turned slightly and jogged his ankle against a sharp stalagmite.

He might have cried out then had not

the grinning girl scampered past him, blank-eyed; it was what she carried that made him choke. He knew what the next stage in the ceremony was. Alfred Douglas had mentioned it.

' . . . the Misguided Wretches who desecrate Christian burial grounds in order to Possess themselves of one of the Foul appurtenances of their feasts . . . '

Jerry saw Brenda's congratulatory grin as the girl presented her prize. It was a withered human hand. Jerry knew now what the sharp cracking noise in the tunnel had been: knew too that this most awful symbol of the Old Religion would be fashioned by the clever educated hands of the schoolgirls.

Brenda signed to two of her acolytes, and they moved forward at her command. They took the rough tapers from her and wired them to the hand, which Jerry had last seen attached to the corpse of the unfortunate Signals lieutenant.

The Hand of Glory took shape. Now each of the large bony fingers were lengthened by the dull-brown tapers, and the wrist embedded in a socket before the altar.

Brenda herself lit the tapers.

Thick, stinking fumes came from the awful Hand.

The fumes were affecting the girls now; a thick yellow-red cloud drifted in the slight eddies of wind that had been set up by the rapid movement of oiled bodies; and the schoolgirls, already dazed and entranced by Brenda's herbs, were swaying as the sulphur further stupefied them and released their inhibitions.

And still the terrible Hand of Glory burnt vividly before the altar. *What next?*

A sign from Brenda brought the entranced pupils of Langdene Academy to a halt. All was in place. The altar had been re-erected. The Hand of Glory flared satisfactorily.

Brenda held both hands high before the terrible devil-mask, and the girls stood straight and tall with a statue's stillness and silence.

A deep and authoritative voice rang out from the lorry-girl's corded throat:

'The waiting is over' The Hour of

release is upon us!'

A long sigh from the girls' throats answered her.

'Magister!'

'He comes!' the harsh, masculine voice reassured them. There was a terrible promise in Brenda's call. 'He comes at the Hour!'

Midnight! Jerry knew the moment had come. *The Devil's Hour!*

How soon midnight had come! Midnight on Walpurgisnacht was when all the terrible astral forces of the Universe could lock on to the psychic imbalance set up in the Coven! All the drugs, all the oils and flickering lights, all the horrid symbols of devil-mask and burning Hand were used for this one reason: to create the frenzied conditions for the legions of the damned to walk abroad! The Black Angel could appear when the souls of the witches were in a proper alignment between ecstasy and evil! But what else had to be done before the ceremony was complete?

What else?

He was distracted from his thoughts by a sudden flurry of movement from the altar. He must have missed a signal, for the girls were moving once again with their familiar robot-like economy of effort.

So far, they had not deigned to look at the long-dead assemblage that had sat at the massive table for over two hundred years.

But the soot-streaked, entranced girls were facing the long table now. Brenda motioned once again, and two of them advanced towards the long-chinned corpse of Lord Titus Brindley.

What did they want with it?

The four girls had hold of the heavy chair in which Lord Titus had rested for several lifetimes. They moved it with easy strength, one at each corner. And turned it to face the flaring Hand!

Then more girls came as Brenda beckoned, and Jerry watched in disbelief as they moved the corpse of the long-dead Satanist from the chair.

Jerry knew a vicarious thrill of horror. How could these delicate schoolgirls bring themselves to handle that withered corpse! How was it that the rough drugs

Brenda had given them could hold them in this state of possession? These carefully-nurtured English roses were now gently stripping the clothes from the gaunt body of Lord Titus Brindley. Why didn't the glowing green corpse affright them?

And why did Julie have to help in laying the almost fluorescent body on to the stone altar slab where the frightful Hand shot yellow and red flame and smoke to the roof of the cavern! Surely, the stench of the long-dead corpse would make her reel with loathing?

And in God's Name what were they doing with the withered corpse!

Amanda was bringing the coalscuttle. Through the swirling clouds of smoke, Jerry could see her plainly; she was smiling.

The black miasmic cloud that hung just over the canopy was waiting with a terrible patience!

'No!' The word forced itself from Jerry's white lips. 'Not that!'

The withered, gaunt corpse of Lord Titus Brindley lay on the altar — one foot grotesquely deformed — and around the withered body clustered the eager young girls; and they were allowing their delicate, middle-class hands to trail over the frightful green cadaver in the caressing action he associated with Brenda's subtle touch on the brass coalscuttle!

Amanda offered the smoking brass cauldron. They squealed with delight and dipped their hands in it.

'Jesus!' groaned Jerry, unable to go to their aid, unwilling to risk a closer acquaintance with the cadaver they were anointing with the mixture of herbs and Vaseline.

'Soon, Magister!' Brenda's unnatural voice rang out. 'The Hour is Now!'

And the girls worked on, industriously oiling the dried and withered corpse!

But why them? Jerry felt fear, and wonder. What had Alfred Douglas said about the use of young girls? Yes! He had it now!

' . . . and the good Rector of Hagthorpe was convinced that the most Efficacious Kind of spell or Conjuration could be Manufactured only when a Girl of Tender

Years was Introduced into the Coven . . . '
Sober and lucid, Davenant had been too much of a Gentleman to introduce the term *virgin* into his journal.

The girls were almost in a frenzy by this time. Brenda stood, tall and ecstatic, facing the corpse. Above the canopy, dim shadows formed momentarily.

'Soon!' warned Brenda.

The girls' efforts redoubled. Amanda joined in the basting of Lord Brindley. Julie slapped the withered skin, forcing the magical preparation through to the flesh below.

Above the canopy, Jerry saw, there was a shape. Vast and black-edged, the form of something recognisable began to emerge.

Brenda called for attention:

'The Lord comes!'

'Yes?'

The girls were incredulous. Their efforts had been rewarded. Jerry heard them chattering congratulations to one another.

Didn't they know what they had brought down on themselves?

'Grey Mentor of the Soul!' called Brenda, and her voice was not a South Yorkshire lorry-girl's, but a deep and resonant voice of command. 'Lord of Darkness, come to me!'

Above the canopy, there was an eddy of smoke. Jerry saw a great pair of eyes flash in the grey emptiness of the cavern, glaring red eyes that hung like brilliant lamps in the darkness of a bestial face.

'Satanus, come to your servant!' grated Brenda's awful voice. 'I bring a sacrifice!'

Without looking at the dozen naked girls at her feet she made a slight movement of one tattooed hand. Julie got to her feet in one swift shining movement, her eyes wet with tears of happiness.

She stepped to the table, with its rotted feast and rows of green cadavers. She lifted the basket and stepped lightly to the altar.

Something yipped in protest.

The vast face above the canopy became more distinct. Brenda, eyes on it, was exultant:

'Lord of the Night! Prince of Darkness! Come!'

'Come!' whispered the middle-class witches. 'Oh, come!'

Jerry felt a roaring in the ears. He knew that he should stay in command of his senses — that he should be ready to act, to do something to help the poor possessed girls. But what?

Yip-yip-yip-yip!

He was about to faint when he heard the noise of the white poodle bitch. It was aware that it was surrounded by enemies! Jerry looked hard through the smoke and saw Julie trying to drag the desolate poodle from the basket.

'The Sacrifice!' Brenda called. 'Come back to us, Magister! Satanus comes when the Sacrifice is made!'

Julie had the struggling poodle bitch now. Strong, capable, pony-girl's hands took Sukie by the scrawny neck and the thin rump. And what was that in Brenda's hand?

Jerry saw the flash of steel.

A kitchen knife! It was the knife he had used to slit open the journal of Alfred Dougas Davenant. And it was to be used to slit open Mrs. Raybould's yipping and snarling pet!

Julie grinned as she held the bitch. Then she advanced to the stone slab where the long cadaver rested greenly. Another girl came forward eagerly at Brenda's signal. Together the two girls held Sukie out like some butcher's carcass, each taking a front and back leg. Sukie looked her astonishment and howled her grief.

'Blood for Satanus!' Brenda called. 'Blood for the Magister!'

Magister? Of course! Master, when translated from the Latin. Magister was —

Lord Titus Brindley!

Jerry knew exactly what Brenda intended now! He knew the reason for her cries to Satanus and the Magister! Lord Titus Brindley was the Master she called upon — Lord Titus, who had been waiting for two centuries for this conjunction of events! Lord Titus, who had been the focus of most terrible emanations during the time he had lain in the cavern called Hag Hole! Powerful forces had been at work trying to gain his release — fantastic and evil forces that had lured the poor Boy Scouts into Hag Hole; frightful emissions of elemental power that had turned the Nazi bomber off course so that it could deposit its bomb-load on the Castle and pave the way for the landslips that eventually cleared the way from the cellar to the cavern! Jerry understood it all now.

Brindley had been the most efficacious black magician since the Dark Ages: his liaison with Satan had not ceased when he had perished in Hag Hole! Some fearful pact must have been enacted between awesome Prince and terrible servant!

But so far nothing had been accomplished! Whatever mysterious astral forces had brought the Heinkel smashing on to Devil's Peak had not been enough to gain freedom for the Brindleys. Though the Castle had been obliterated, the awesome and Satanic powers had been misdirected! No Boy Scouts' penknife or Signals Lieutenant's tool-kit had been enough either to release the Coven! The poor wretches who had been lured into Hag Hole had even tried to gnaw through to the Brindleys in their desperate possessed state! But the forces of evil had been blind, undirected, and ineffective, until Brenda took the initiative! Until Brenda cast her terrible spell on the schoolgirls!

The Brindleys had lain waiting until the psychic forces released by the twelve virgins were in readiness. And Brenda would enable the Grand Master of the Coven to lead them to a most horrid awakening! Jerry felt sick. Brenda was utterly dedicated to her task. All her short and strange life had been a preparation for her inherited mission. She was come to the cavern so that Satan's priest could live again! Jerry watched the blade of the knife, mesmerised by its flashing menace.

The poodle yipped only feebly now, for it could sense the great and gathering miasma of evil above the canopy. The thing had a form that mocked the human shape. There was a broad, hairy face, with eyes of violent red coals; shoulders that sloped forward, and a vicious stench emanated from the Shape, foul and horrible! The sulphurous fumes from the terrifying Hand and the waves of foetid corruption from the gloating figure above made Jerry retch; bile flooded into his mouth, and he had to turn to spit it out. Something beneath him jabbed sharply into his side.

He felt cautiously beneath his body and dragged the obstruction out of his anorak pocket. The candles he had taken from the Mountain Rescue boxes. He pushed them away from him. As he did so, the green cadaver on the stone slab arched upwards.

'He comes!' screamed Brenda.

'Yes!' the girls screamed back, exhausted by joy and tremulous excitement.

'The Hour!' screamed Brenda, and Jerry saw that the long-dead, emaciated cadaver had moved!

He shuddered. His fingers clutched at something by the stalagmites that screened him: he gripped hard on the candles — candles? — he had pushed away. But they were made of cardboard. One small part of his mind considered the information supplied by his fingers; the rest was overwhelmed by a surge of great horror, for withered arms moved upwards.

Worse followed!

Lord Titus' long skinny hands moved out to encompass the screaming miniature poodle.

Brenda abased herself at this sign of resurgent life and authority. The two schoolgirls released the unhappy white bitch to the dead man's arms and followed Brenda to their knees. The sacrifice would be completed by the Magister!

Above, the vast Shape was almost formed. There was a thick torso, gnarled like a huge oak, and covered in greasy tufts of thick hair. The face was a straining mask of pure malicious delight; yellow fangs glimmered in the flaring sulphur flames; sharp, curved horns glinted awkwardly. The terrible apparition bent to inspect the offering below.

'Satanus!' whispered Brenda.

Lord Titus Brindley, clasping the whimpering form of Sukie to his gaunt chest, creaked to his feet. The withered, dry flesh shone with oil. And then Jerry saw the face, greenly glowing, greenly alive. There was an expression of intense hatred combined with flaring hope on the dried flesh. His eyes shone through the smoke, anticipating the sacrifice.

'Don't!' Jerry implored as the green cadaver got to its feet.

He whispered the words from the journal: 'Deliver this Thy servant from Unclean Spirits! But would God act? Would a Sword of Fire appear?'

'Save me from the Venomous Serpent,' Jerry said, as Brenda placed the kitchen knife on the altar and reached her ancestor's reactivated body.

There was a dead silence in the cavern.

The skinny arms lifted Sukie high. The knife glittered on the altar.

There was a rush of indrawn breath near Jerry.

For a moment he thought that some angelic presence had manifested itself to confront the forces of evil. He jerked to look towards the cavern door. It was a woman.

'Sukie-darling!'

'Mrs. Raybould!' Jerry gasped.

Couldn't she see what was happening!

Didn't she recognise her danger!

Mrs. Raybould appeared quite oblivious of the frightful scene before her. She stood just inside the cavern, peering into the smoke-filled interior with no hint that she saw what it contained.

Jerry heard a groan from the canopy, and with it the creaking of old, long-dead bones.

'Satanus!' rumbled the voice of Lord Titus Brindley.

'Sukie!' called Mrs. Raybould.

Then Jerry saw that she was fumbling in her apron pocket for her spectacles. The Hand flared in a last furious efflorescence before the tapers were consumed. Sukie heard Mrs. Raybould and yipped for her life.

'Sukie!' Mrs. Raybould yelled, spectacles on her long nose.

'Sukie-what's-she-found-now!' she reproved.

Above the canopy, the vast goat's head grinned. Brenda saw Mrs. Raybould, and a gleam of delight came into her eyes.

'Mrs. Raybould, they'll sacrifice you!' Jerry roared.

Brenda and the girls heard.

They turned, just as Jerry's hands tightened on the cardboard tubes.

What was he doing? He was hobbling towards the table, after Mrs. Raybould!

Brenda and the girls watched Mrs. Raybould walk, blinking, to the altar.

The frightful cadaver held Sukie high.

Then Brenda yelled: 'Get her!'

The awesome corpse turned, with the poodle bitch yipping frantically in its dried, bony hands.

'Who are you?' Mrs. Raybould called. 'That's my Sukie!'

'The Sacrifice!' croaked the emaciated skull.

'Yes!' Brenda screamed.

'Yes!' the girls echoed, getting to their feet.

'No!' Jerry bawled.

'You shouldn't be down here!' Mrs. Raybould reproved. 'Sukie, get down!'

Sukie bit hard, wriggled and, summoning all her frail strength, launched her thin body on to the long table. The green cadaverous figure groaned once more, and Jerry could see a kind of life in its horrid, decayed eyes. But it was not intelligence, not yet! Only a fearsome elemental force was in that body. The ceremony would not be completely successful without a sacrifice. And here was poor, idiotic Mrs. Raybould offering herself to these malevolent creatures! Even as she reached for Sukie, the girls were around her, oiled bodies gleaming with young muscle!

Jerry paused. What in God's name could he do?

'Burn them, Lord!' he whispered, but words, however comforting, were ineffective. He gripped on the cardboard tubes.

Ideas raced through his mind. *Throw them?* To what effect? He raised his hand and saw what he had picked out of the Mountain Rescue box,

Flares!

He could make his own Sword of Fire! Arthur Douglas had told him what to do!

In each hand he held a powerful flare, which could burn at a huge temperature and whose vast flames could be seen for miles! He had a weapon! Fire against Evil! Light against Darkness! The Flames of the Sword of Fire against the

Venomous Serpent!

'Satanus!' groaned the voice of the black magician, a world of imploring hopelessness in its tone.

'Don't touch her!' Jerry yelled. 'Don't or — '

He stopped.

Brenda stared, fire-dark eyes full of a great hatred; the vicious smile-snarl on her face was reflected on each one of the girls' faces. They knew he could not harm them.

Then the cadaver was moving. It held out withered arms for the sacrifice. And it took the glittering knife from the altar.

'Get off to your beds!' Mrs. Raybould whimpered, struggling against disbelief. 'It's not nice down there!'

The cadaver took a step towards her. Jerry heard the clump of a heavy boot — Brindley's club-foot — on the rock floor.

Then he acted, almost for the first time in his life, without conscious thought. What he intended — what he tried to do — was to save the woman. First he stooped and rubbed the end of each flare on the ground: immediately both powerful flares were alight, red wholesome light bursting from the cardboard tubes. Then he rushed at the terrible green corpse.

He was ten paces or so away, but it took him a second or two to get into a stumbling and painful run.

'Satanus!' bawled the corpse. There was a glimmer of understanding in the decayed eyes. Jerry held the flares out.

'No!' shrieked Brenda.

Overhead, a rumbling shook the cavern, and a stench of filth and detritus filled the air; the Hand of Glory guttered down. Jerry sensed that he was the mark for forces of evil too horrifying to dream of. Cold dankness hovered above him in a coiled mass.

The cadaver saw Jerry's run. It staggered to meet him, face straining with the effort to clutch this new offering to its withered torso. The girls ran towards Jerry's side of the table, crying out in a frenzy. They ignored Mrs. Raybould and her poodle. Brenda's arms were raised high as she shrieked for help,

'King of Darkness!' she implored. 'Come down to us!'

The cold clammy air almost stifled Jerry. He saw a cluster of dreadful slimy things, hovering near the green, creaking corpse. They fled as he waved a brilliant red flare high.

He was full of a great jubilation now. He had acted, and whatever the outcome he had conquered that weakness Debbie had despised so much. He had faced the Adversary!

Then he kicked against a chair leg, gasped with pain, and went down.

The cadaver loomed above him. High-pitched, well-educated voices yipped with pleasure. Brenda shouted a threat. Sukie howled in fright.

Jerry saw the club-foot. There was a short, mouldy shank, a twisted ankle, and a slimy contraption of leather and rusted iron about the foot.

He was sick to the soul, yet his new-found courage did not desert him. Somehow he had kept one flare in his right hand.

In agonizing pain, he lashed out with

his good foot at the rotted and rusted contraption on the revived magician's foot. Immediately it gave, and the cadaver keeled over.

Jerry pushed out his hand to ward off the collapsing corpse. Withered tissue jarred against his hand; and then the cadaver let out an appalling roar of anguish. Jerry saw why.

Stiff with terror, gulping air frantically, retching at the nearness of the long-dead body, Jerry understood the reason for the great booming roar from the black magician's shrivelled throat.

The blazing flare was stuck in the two-centuries old flesh! The flames and gases ate into the withered flanks. The Sword of Fire had transfixed him!

'Satanus, help your servant!' the long-dead creature groaned.

But the flames had found the well-vaselined skin, and Lord Titus was a mass of blue and red flame!

Jerry rolled aside, clear of the table and its cold assemblage. The girls were watching helplessly as the ancient corpse staggered to its feet, covered in fire.

246

Brenda screamed with rage, seeking the assistance of the snarling beast above. But it was uninterested now!

'Come out, come out!' Mrs. Raybould shouted, as if oblivious of the eerie sight. 'You should all be in your beds! It isn't right!'

Jerry got to his feet in considerable pain.

'Magister!' screamed Brenda, but Lord Titus ignored her. Flame came from his white hair, from all over his body, even from his mouth. And behind him, burning its all-consuming way into the dried-up organs of his body, the bright red flame surged on.

'It's over! You've failed!' Jerry shouted m triumph.

The girls fell back as he retrieved the other flare, which still burnt as fiercely as the one embedded in Lord Titus.

'Stop him!' yelled Brenda.

But Jerry Howard could not be stopped — would not be stopped.

He reached out to another of the Brindleys and fired a mop of brown hair, then he set light to a mouldy coat. then another, then another; clothing, dry flesh, ancient hair, all flamed up brightly.

'No!' screamed Brenda. She looked up. 'Satanus, come down! Destroy the unbeliever!'

Jerry grinned at her. He could feel the heat of bright, wholesome, evil-destroying fire as it pushed aside the cold clammy things above. He kicked over the guttering Hand of Glory and grabbed the cauldron of still-liquid oil.

'Get back to bed!' he shouted to the girls. 'She's not your mistress now!'

'Don't!' Brenda begged, as Jerry launched the oil over the table. It ran on to the laps of the burning Brindleys, intensifying the blaze.

'It's the Devil's birthday, isn't it?' Jerry shouted. 'You need candles at a birthday party!'

He was beside himself, intoxicated with relief from fear. He was in an insane delirium of joy, strength and arrogance.

Julie was the first to blink out of her hallucinated condition. She gasped as she saw the flames.

'Oh!' she screamed as she realised that she was naked.

The girls hid their breasts and ran.

Brenda stood in the cavern weeping at the sight of the mass incineration of her clan.

It took several minutes for Sam Raybould and Bill Ainsley to convince him that they should not join the Brindleys, for Jerry was become a pyromaniac. Twice he tried to set light to them.

At last Jerry calmed down and recognised the two men.

'We came back to see how you was getting on,' said Raybould.

'*I'm* all right!'

There was a satisfying crackling of flame as the canopy came down. Brenda was sobbing in Bill Ainsley's comforting arms. The big red face of the lorry-driver cracked into a grin.

'All right now, Brenda. No harm done! There's a thaw come outside — we can go early!'

Jerry's exultation left him when he saw her terrible, fire-dark eyes. They were full of undying hatred. He shivered and dropped the shell of the flare. The girl was struggling to say something.

'Hush, now, Brenda!' ordered Bill. 'You need your sleep, lass!'

Still the girl's eyes were on Jerry. He wished that he had burned her too. She whispered at him:

' . . . He will avenge the Magister!'

'Well, what's been going on here?' the café-owner demanded, realising that he was in no danger.

'Well,' said Jerry, conscious of the fearsome, hating eyes, 'there was a bit of an accident.' Then as he left the cavern, his courage asserted itself once more. 'Happy Birthday!' he shouted at the smouldering ruins and glowing long-dead bones. 'Happy Bloody Birthday!'

14

Jerry didn't tell Debbie about the events of Walpurgisnacht until a month after their marriage at the South Shields Registry Office. He had left the caff at first light, hitched a lift to Leeds and then on to Shields where Debbie was in bed at her parents' little terraced house. He had hammered on the door until she came down — beautiful, big, loud-voiced, sleepy-eyed, bosomy, furious — and then he had ordered her back to bed where he immediately joined her. It was fortunate for him that they were caught there by Debbie's mother who had returned to collect her forgotten sandwiches (she worked in a local factory). A wild row culminated in an order for instant matrimony which, duly accomplished, led to a reappraisal of Jerry's career.

He had been a bingo-hall executive for three weeks when he saw the picture in the *Daily Mirror*.

It was Brenda.

He flipped his teacup over his scrambled eggs. Debbie looked up from the *Financial Times*.

'You'll be late.'

'It's her!'

'Who?' Debbie was fully awake now. She had not loved the trawler man: all her passion had been for Jerry Howard. And all of his would be for her.

'Brenda!'

'Who's she?'

'A witch!'

Debbie yawned. 'Don't be silly — that's all nonsense!' She broke off at his expression, and leant over to take his now shaking hands.

'What's the matter, love?'

Jerry told her.

When he had finished, she poured him more tea. 'Drink it up. Don't bother going in till late.'

Jerry stared at the picture. Whippet-thin, pretty eyes, pretty lips, set in that mockery of a smile! But so elegantly clad!

Brenda had come up in the world!

'It's worrying you, isn't it?' said

Debbie. 'You should have told me earlier.'

'I hoped nothing would ever come out! I never read a word about it.'

'Nothing? I remember hearing about the girls trapped at the caff. Didn't they say anything about this black magic business?'

'Not a word! Next morning they didn't remember it at all! They'd got headaches, but they didn't seem to have been affected in any other way — there was a total loss of memory, amnesia, so far as that Brindley business was concerned.'

'What about the others?'

'Bill and Brenda didn't say anything either. And the Rayboulds didn't want the publicity!'

'But there must have been some evidence! All those bodies! Didn't the police investigate?'

Jerry crossed to the new Scandinavian bureau, which had been his parents' wedding-present. He took out the journal of Alfred Douglas Davenant.

'That's all there is to see.'

He remembered the thunder in the

night, the underground rumblings and swirlings.

'Nothing else?'

The thaw did it. The river opened up again when the snow melted — everything was cleaned out. The cellars were flooded, the tunnel and the cavern simply scoured out. Bill went down early next morning with me. All the corpses were gone! Every speck of dust, every bone, every bit of equipment, was gone too. So what could we say?'

Debbie was reading the journal.

'What do you think, Deb? Should I have stayed? I mean, to get the police in?'

She looked up. 'And not come for me! Don't be bloody silly, love!'

Jerry sighed with relief. He stared at the picture until Debbie, noticing his continued attention, took the paper.

'She looks a witch,' she said. 'Did you read the caption?'

Jerry hadn't. The familiar evil smile had hypnotised him.

'She's getting married. ' — Here's a secret smile from Miss Brenda Brindley' — '

'She *is* a Brindley!'

' ' — who met her fiancé, Mr. Rupert Mauleverer, at an M1 café only three weeks ago! After a whirlwind courtship, the couple decided to marry at once! There's romance on the roads, girls! Mr. Mauleverer is a director of the Restsecure Cryogenics Foundation, so — '

'What!' Jerry gulped. 'That word — cryo — ?'

'Cryogenics. They keep corpses on ice. Until they want to revive them, that is.'

Jerry fumbled with the newspaper. 'The bitch! She's at it again!'

Debbie's face was pale. 'A witch,' she whispered. 'Is she?'

Debbie got to her feet and crossed to the tray where letters were thrown.

'The bitch!' she said again. She passed an opened envelope across to Jerry. 'It came last week. I thought it was a circular.'

Jerry took out the sheet of paper apprehensively. His fingers shook as he saw the printed, bold type:

'Restsecure Brings You a New Concept in Life After Death! Your Body can be

Kept In a Hermetically-Sealed Vault in Hygienic Conditions Until At Some Time In the Future You Are Restored by Advances in Medicine! Why Not Call At Our Manchester Office — '

'Dear Christ!' Jerry whispered, suddenly cold. He looked at the journal. It had fallen open at the prayer.

He and Debbie stared in fright at one another. Then their gaze went to the leaflet again. For, written at the bottom in an uneducated scrawl was a message of doom:

'I'll be waiting. Long Life!'

Finally, Jerry whispered: 'If anything does happen to me — '

'It won't!'

But Jerry was afraid of more than death; he had to make sure of this. *Had* to be sure that Brenda would not imperil his soul!

They looked back to the expensively-printed leaflet and its scrawl.

Jerry had to be sure.

'If it does, don't let her get her hands on me. Please? *Please!*'

We do hope that you have enjoyed reading this large print book.

Did you know that all of our titles are available for purchase?

We publish a wide range of high quality large print books including:
Romances, Mysteries, Classics
General Fiction
Non Fiction and Westerns

Special interest titles available in large print are:
The Little Oxford Dictionary
Music Book, Song Book
Hymn Book, Service Book

Also available from us courtesy of Oxford University Press:
Young Readers' Dictionary
(large print edition)
Young Readers' Thesaurus
(large print edition)

For further information or a free brochure, please contact us at:
Ulverscroft Large Print Books Ltd.,
The Green, Bradgate Road, Anstey,
Leicester, LE7 7FU, England.
Tel: (00 44) **0116 236 4325**
Fax: (00 44) **0116 234 0205**

Other titles in the
Linford Mystery Library:

THE MURDERED SCHOOLGIRL

John Russell Fearn

Maria Black, Head of Roseway College for Young Ladies, and solver of crimes, is faced with a problem after her own heart when young Frances Hasleigh arrives at the college. Within days the girl is found hanged in a neighbouring wood, in circumstances that seem to be devoid of clues and without motive. When Scotland Yard is called in, Maria applies her own unique system to find a way through a maze of intrigue — and uncovers the murderer . . .